CHaPTer
one

A NEW shimmery violet eye shadow, highlighted with a dusty gray, covered my eyelids. I cocked my head from side to side, watching my reflection in the mirror as the stream of light from the desk lamp caused the new makeup to sparkle. It was bold, daring, and in my opinion, totally kick-ass cool. With a steady, practiced hand, I added a heavy line of smoky eyeliner around each eye in a winged pattern. Thick penciled-in eyebrows with a high arch, a dab of blush to each cheek, and a light layer of gloss over my plum-lined lips completed the look. Damn, I looked good!

"Really, Danny?"

I looked over to see my best friend Bo leaning against the doorframe, arms crossed over his chest. "What? Too much?" I ran my fingers through my purple-streaked blond hair, fluffing it, giving it a little more height.

"Uh, yeah, you could say that." Bo rolled his eyes. "We're going to a frat party, not a rave."

"Same diff," I said. Bunch of posturing men, drinking and flexing their muscles as they chased after one conquest or another. The only difference was that at a frat house, the beer would be free and the dance floor for shit. Turning away from an exasperated Bo—I knew that expression on his face well—I grabbed the can of hairspray from the makeshift vanity and gave my hair another couple of blasts of the extra sticky hold. Once I was satisfied every hair was in perfect place and would be able to withstand forty-mile-an-hour wind gusts, I set the can down and turned back to face Bo.

Bo waved a hand in my direction. "And what the hell are you wearing?"

I looked down at my attire and shrugged. Torn and frayed jeans hung low on my lean hips, held in place by a black belt with silver studs. Heavy-soled black lace-up knee boots were hidden behind faded denim so only the black matte leather of the toe was visible. A vintage black Rolling Stones T-shirt, with the classic lips and protruding tongue displayed on the front, completed my ensemble. I hadn't even added any of the numerous leather and silver bracelets I normally wore on each wrist, no collar or any other jewelry except the diamond stud in my right ear. If anything, I was underdressed.

"What do you mean?" I arched one perfectly penciled brow at him. "Not macho enough?"

Bo threw his head back and laughed. "You look like a punch-drunk drag queen."

"Fuck off!" I mumbled, but laughed along with him. *Punch-drunk drag queen. Whatever!*

Stifling my giggles, I ran a critical eye down Bo's slim body. Boot-cut, dark-wash denim jeans, white, dollar-store tennis shoes, faded blue-and-white-striped polo shirt. One word came to mind: *boring* and *cheap*. Okay, that was two words, but both were accurate. "Better than the thrifty-geek look you're going for."

When Bo and I stood side by side, our differences were glaringly obvious, like night and day. He's the conservative one, while I've always had a flair for theatrics and love being the center of attention. No one was surprised when I decided to attend the University of Michigan as a theater major—what had surprised some was that I'd dragged Bo along with me. Bo and I were not only roommates but had been best friends since junior high. They say opposites attract and in this case, the saying was certainly true.

Bo's real name is Bogart Humphrey, a cruel joke his parents played on him at birth and I promised to keep that secret since I was thirteen, under threat of having my head and eyebrows shaved while I slept. I never told anyone Bo's real name, as even seven years later, baldness was still a very real possibility.

Whispering Pines Ranch by SJD PETERSON

Lorcan's Desire

"Get a box of Kleenex and settle in for a stormy ride. It is totally worth it." —Mrs. Condit & Friends

"In short, SJD Peterson rocked the angst, and I loved every word of it." —Top 2 Bottom Reviews

Quinn's Need

"OH wow this was a franticly hot book." —Musings of a Bookworm

"This book is brilliant, the storyline is fantastic, the characters are incredible…." —MM Good Book Reviews

Ty's Obsession

"These books are all beautifully written, and this third novel is filled with scenes that illustrate that overarching reality of sensitive and authentic love that these men share." —Book Binge

"The cast of Whispering Pines is dynamic and will draw you in, making you crave more." —Guilty Pleasures Book Reviews

Conner's Courage

"This book is amazing. Beautifully written, believably paced and just so honest and true." —A Bear on Books

By SJD PETERSON

<u>NOVELS</u>

WHISPERING PINES RANCH
Lorcan's Desire
Quinn's Need
Ty's Obsession
Conner's Courage
Jess's Journey

Masters & Boyd

Published by DREAMSPINNER PRESS
http://www.dreamspinnerpress.com

PLAN B
SJD Peterson

Dreamspinner Press

Published by
Dreamspinner Press
5032 Capital Circle SW
Ste 2, PMB# 279
Tallahassee, FL 32305-7886
USA
http://www.dreamspinnerpress.com/

Plan B

Cover art by Ronaldo Gutierrez, Photographer
Cover design by Paul Richmond

ISBN: 978-1-62380-337-7
Digital ISBN: 978-1-62380-338-4

Printed in the United States of America
First Edition
February 2013

For everyone who is deemed different.
Don't try to fit in, be you. *STAND OUT!*

Bo is tall, a good five inches taller than my own five foot eight inches. He has mousy-brown hair always cut short and parted on the side, wire-rimmed glasses, and had a penchant for shopping at Goodwill for the most dull, nondescript clothing he could find. While I loved makeup, fashion, Broadway, dancing, and visiting art museums, Bo loved math, studied business, and was most comfortable hiding behind me in public—despite our size difference. He was happiest either watching *Star Trek* reruns or hanging out at conventions with his fellow *Trek* fans. However, no matter the differences, we'd grown up virtually inseparable since Bo moved into the house next door to mine. We were both only children, the only two boys around the same age in our neighborhood, and for some odd reason, we just worked as friends. One of the most interesting dynamics of our relationship was, as flippant and flamboyant as I was, he accepted me. We didn't always like the same things, but we took turns and kept score on whose turn it was to pick the entertainment, be it club or restaurant.

While I was always speaking my mind, often times without the assistance of a filter between brain and mouth, Bo tended to be more reserved and quiet, at least until someone disrespected someone he cared about. He'd go from the shy, nerdy guy to the puffed-up protector whenever anyone threw a derogatory slur my way. Bo was raised to be a truly great person, and I loved him unconditionally. I knew he felt the same, but that didn't mean I didn't like to tease the shit out of him whenever the opportunity arose.

Bo didn't say anything else about my appearance, knowing it was a fruitless effort to try to get me to conform to the ideology of normalcy. Normal—whatever that meant—was mundane, and if there is one thing Daniel Anderson Marshal is not, it is boring. I refused to dress like the masses in an effort to "fit in." Sure, I took some ribbing for it, a few nasty insults tossed my way here and there when I walked by, even had some old guy ask me if I was a boy or girl. I answered by cupping the bulge in my pink skinny jeans and asking, "Would you like me to show you?" Did I also mention that I was a major smartass at times? I loved the shock and wow factor. I don't think I've ever seen anyone that old move away so fast or turn so red. No matter what reaction I got, I'd still rather be an individual dressing the way I want, than a sheep that follows the rest of the crowd.

To prove this point, I grabbed my new white, waist-length coat with black fur trim around the hood and slipped it on. Yes, I'd bought it in the junior girls' section and I fucking loved it. All soft and snuggly. Loved the way the fur felt around my face when I put up the hood. I'm a very tactile, as well as visual, guy.

"Okay, now I'm ready."

"Don't forget your Hello Kitty purse," Bo said, brushing past me to grab his simple tan golf jacket from the back of his desk chair.

"Tsk, tsk," I chastised. "How many times do I have to tell you, the Hello Kitty purse matches the pink fur boots, not the black gothic punk boots?" I pushed out my hip and placed a hand on it. "Jeez, Bo, can't you even remember that fashion simplicity? Oh. My. God! Bag must match the footwear," I told him overly dramatically and then stomped my foot to complete the effect. "Always."

Bo suddenly stopped with his coat midway up his arms, eyes wide. "You don't actually have one, do you?"

I just rolled my eyes at him as I stepped out of our dorm room. No, I didn't have a Hello Kitty anything—the yellow boyshorts with the black outline of a popular kitty doesn't count, since I'd never actually worn them, they were a gift—or a pair of pink fur boots, I considered going on a little shopping trip, just to drive Bo crazy, but there was no way I was wearing kitty anything. Bo complained about my antics sometimes, but I knew he liked them. I kept him from living a slow, painfully humdrum existence. Secretly I think he lived vicariously through me.

I SET my boot on the first step leading up to the frat house and my nerves made themselves known by the jittery feeling in my stomach. I took a deep breath and squared my shoulders for the shit storm about to be unleashed. I hated frat parties. Add me to a cesspool of alcohol, combine a few alpha jocks, and stir in a little macho bullshit, and it's a recipe for disaster. However, Bo was pining after some chick who would be there, and since he'd also grudgingly attended the ballet with me, I owed him.

Stopping on the top step, hand on the doorknob, I looked over my shoulder at Bo. "She better be worth it," I warned, then cocked my head and gave him another onceover. I sighed exaggeratedly. "And take off that butt-ass-ugly grandpa coat or you'll never get the chance to find out if she is or not."

Ignoring the incoherent grumbling from Bo, I opened the door and stepped inside. I was hit with a thick cloud of smoke, my eyes instantly began to water, and the stench of cigarettes, alcohol and pot hung cloyingly in the air. It made me nauseated, and I wrinkled my nose in disgust. My pulse pounded along with the loud music blasting from crap speakers. I use the word *music* lightly here, since I had no idea what song was playing—the distortion made it nothing more than a thumping bass of noise.

"You owe me," I mouthed to Bo.

Bo nodded, shucked out of his coat, and hurried past me, disappearing into the throng of partygoers, no doubt on the hunt for his love interest. After walking over in temperatures in the thirties, the room felt stuffy, and I removed my own coat and tucked it under my arm. *Might as well find a drink and a quiet corner*. I sighed and hoped Bo would either hook up with his honey and I'd be able to sneak out before too long, or better yet, Bo would discover she wasn't here and wasn't coming and we could get the hell out of Dodge.

Many of the classier fraternity houses around campus, like the Greek houses, tended to be turn-of-the-century homes, eloquent with nice furnishings and stone fireplaces. Even the low-key frat houses were nice, reflecting the type of people who comprise the fraternity. I was beginning to suspect this place wasn't even a fraternity, but rather a big party house. There were no insignias hung on the dingy gray walls; the furniture was mismatched and torn. Hell, even the Deltas in *Animal House* had fucking insignias. This place was just a big, nasty stinkfest. I'd seen boarded up and abandoned houses that looked better than this. The only difference was this dump had electricity.

As I made my way farther into the room, one guy openly sneered at me while another looked at me with a confused expression. Some of the females stared with the same questioning look minus the sneer, others pointed and giggled, and still others examined me with obvious interest. I ignored them all. My only concern at that point was finding the keg, having a beer, and trying to figure out how long I had to stay before I'd fulfilled my obligation to Bo.

I covered my nose with the back of my hand as I moved into the dining room. Unbelievably, the stench was worse in here. The worn and matted carpet hadn't seen a broom or a vacuum in years. The peeling wallpaper was filthy; a nasty yellow film covered it. The odor of stale beer, sweat, and what I suspected was the sour smell of vomit was strong enough to overpower the nasty stink of smoke. From the twenty-plus people crowding around the beer pong table, it was a popular hangout, despite the disgusting conditions. I couldn't help but think, *How the fuck can you people stand this?* But I didn't ponder it long. Nausea made the saliva pool in my mouth, and I lengthened my steps. I had to get out of there before I ended up adding to the upchuck smell. Bo's lust interest may have had a good reason to be there, but I still planned to kill Bo for making me come.

I forced my way past the crowd. Just as I made it into the kitchen and spotted the holy grail of beer—the keg—a tickling sensation started at the base of my neck. The hairs there were literally standing straight up as I was hit with the overwhelming feeling I was being watched, but when I scanned the room around me, I didn't see anyone staring at me.

To my right, there was a girl sitting on the kitchen counter with a dude standing between her spread legs as he devoured her mouth while his hands pawed at her ample breasts. They were really going at it, humping against each other, eyes closed, and moaning. I seriously doubted they were aware of anyone in the room with them, so intent on each other. There was no one to my left, and the view out the window showed a large crowd of people on the back deck. I leaned closer to the scum-covered pane, straining to catch a glimpse of someone looking in my direction, but no one was. Shaking off the uneasy feeling, I rubbed at the back of my neck. I figured it was just the smell finally getting to me. My stomach was still queasy and I felt dizzy. I grabbed a cup from the middle of the stack and filled it with foamy brew.

I took a sip, crazily thrilled that it was cold, turned, and froze. I mean, I just fucking froze with that Solo cup against my lips, breath stuck in my throat when I met bloodshot, steel-gray eyes.

Leaning against the wall in between the dining and kitchen areas, arms across his chest, was a broad, muscular guy, staring at me intently. There wasn't anything extraordinary about the man. I mean, he was good-looking, in that typical all-American jock way, but I'd seen better. He had dark brown hair cut short, and at least two days' growth of stubble on his square jaw and chin, giving him a rugged look. There also wasn't anything remarkable about the way he was dressed—a blue U of M sweatshirt and faded jeans—but his gaze? It was as if he wasn't just looking *at* me, but inside me. As if he could see past the flash, the flesh, and right into the very center of who I was, where I hid my secrets, desires, kinks, all of it. Don't ask me how or why I felt that way just from the look in his eyes, but I did and it freaked me the fuck out.

A shudder ran through me and it was enough to break the spell I seemed to be under and pry my eyes from his. I lowered my cup slowly, a slight tremble in my hand. The stranger didn't say a word, just continued to stare. Although I had lowered my eyes, I could still feel his on me, in me. Totally off-kilter, I gave him a tight smile. "Nice party," I said without looking up. I turned on my heels and hurried out the back door in search of Bo.

I found him sitting on a log in front of a small fire burning in a rock-lined pit. "Way to ditch me, bastard," I complained as I took a seat next to him.

"Sorry about that," Bo muttered, then more enthusiastically said, "This is Katie," as he pointed to a cute red-haired girl next to him. "Katie Lenard, this is my best friend, Danny Marshal."

I reached across Bo and extended my hand. "Hi, Katie. I've heard a lot about you."

Although there was a moonless and starless dark sky above, the fire gave off enough light to see Katie's pale skin flush dark. She accepted my offered hand and shook it. "I've heard a lot about you as well. Nice to finally meet you."

The tone of her voice was meek and matched her size, but for a tiny thing she sure had a firm handshake. She also had a wide, beautiful smile and the flush of her skin highlighted the spattering of freckles across her button nose. She was cute, not flashy, but rather reserved in her barn coat, blue-and-gold scarf, and jeans. I could see why she appealed to Bo. She was quietly beautiful, if that made sense.

The cool fall wind blowing against my back caused me to shiver and I slipped on my coat. "All of it true, I'm sure." I shot Bo a look that said, "You better have told her how great I am." He just smiled.

"So you're a theater major? I love the theater. I would never have the nerve to actually get on a stage, but I love going to watch. I envy you that." Her hands moved wildly as she spoke. "Oh, that is the cutest coat I've ever seen. Where did you get it? And your makeup is beautiful, I mean like, just wow! Your eyeliner is amazing."

Jesus, girl, breathe!

I looked to Bo for some help, but he just continued to smile.

"And your hair, man, I wish I had the confidence to do something that bold. I always plan to get something fun when I go to the beauty shop, but I always chicken out at the last minute. It must take a long time to style it like that. Do you do it yourself?"

Katie's eyes went wide, her face turning a bright shade of red, when Bo chuckled. "Oh God, I'm so sorry. I tend to ramble when I'm nervous." She covered her face with both hands.

"It's okay," I said easily. "Hey, at least you didn't ask if I wanted to be your BFF and invite me over for a pajama party." It annoyed the hell out of me when chicks asked me that. Unfortunately, I'd been asked more than once. Like they think just because I could apply makeup and had a thing for really cool hairstyles, it's enough for them to want me as a best friend. People like that who base their friendships on such superficial crap are morons. My usual response to dipshits like that was "Wouldn't you rather have a puppy to dress up and show off?" But I knew Katie hadn't meant anything; in fact, she was rather complimentary. I did have "the cutest coat ever," and I was "just wow."

She dropped her hands quickly, an appalled expression on her face. "I would never—"

"Katie, he's kidding," Bo assured her. "Although"—he quirked a brow at me—"I think he might be a little disappointed that you didn't want to have a PJ party with him."

"Shut up," I grumbled, the smile lessening the harsh words, and bumped Bo's shoulder.

I was a little nervous at the thought of asking Katie a question, afraid it would send her off on another long-winded chatter, but I didn't want to be rude and I wanted a distraction from the eerie feeling that was still gripping me from the encounter in the kitchen. I set my beer on the ground and zipped up my jacket, before grabbing my cup once again and taking a long pull. "So, Katie. How did you meet this lug?" I nodded toward Bo. "Are you a business major also?"

She looked relieved for the subject change. "Hotel and Restaurant Management. We sit next to each other in ECON class."

Over the next half hour, I sipped on that beer and added a nod and a "yeah" where it seemed appropriate, as Bo and Katie talked about their shared class and professor. But I really didn't care what Professor Steward said or assigned and was only half listening. To be honest, I was bored out of my fucking mind and I figured by the time I finished the now warm brew, I'd have put in a long enough of an appearance to be considered even with Bo for the ballet.

Focusing on the yellow and orange flames as they danced and shot sparks of light upward, I took another sip from my cup and jerked, spilling the remainder of the beer down my front when someone sat next to me, hitting my arm.

"What the hell, you clumsy shit?" I sputtered, wiping the spilled brew from my jacket. I looked over, and for the second time that night, I did a great imitation of a snowman and froze. Sitting next to me, glaring, sat the stranger I'd encountered earlier, and he didn't look as if his mood had improved.

"You bothering my sister?" The man's breath stunk with the stench of alcohol and his words were slightly slurred.

"Lance!" Katie yelled, coming to her feet, the angry tone of her voice grabbing my attention. She placed her hands on her hips, eyes blazing when they landed on her brother.

Brother? Just fucking great!

"No one is bothering me. Now. Go. Away!"

I looked back to—*are you kidding me?*—her brother, only to discover he seemed to be completely ignoring his sister, intently focused on me.

After a long, awkward moment of silence, where the big jock brother burrowed those gray eyes into me with what appeared to be contempt, he asked, "Do you suck dick?"

For what felt like moments but was probably mere seconds, everyone went quiet, frozen, whether in shock, outrage, or confusion as each processed Lance's crude words.

"Lance!" Katie screamed again with outrage, breaking the silence.

Okay, I hadn't seen that one coming, or maybe I did. I get a lot of people making assumptions about me. I guess I could have just responded, "I do, in fact, and quite enjoy it, thank you very much. Do you?" But I was feeling particularly evil considering the way he'd affected me, and let's just say I don't like being unbalanced, shocked, or left speechless, and Lance—really? Her goddamn brother?—had done all three.

"Why? Does my breath smell like dick?"

The jock asshole just stared, his menacing expression turning to confusion.

Bo's hand landed on my forearm. Ignoring Bo's touch and Katie's continuing rant at her brother, I held Lance's gaze. He continued to stare at me without a word, as if he were waiting for me to actually tell him whether or not I did. Each second of silence just stoked my irritation and, I admit, gave me time to throw off the shock and come up with a witty retort.

I cupped my mouth with one hand and inhaled deeply, as if I were attempting to smell my breath. "I thought she tasted funny. That cheating bitch! I'll kill her!" I jumped to my feet and stomped away. Let him try to figure out what the hell that meant. Although the dumbass was probably too stupid.

Whatever. I was out of there.

"Danny, wait!"

I kept walking. God, I hate assholes. What I despise even more than assholes are dipshits who think just because someone is gay, they can ask them anything they want. Be as crude as they want when asking about their sex life. Well fuck that. You never hear anyone ask a checkout girl or their kid's teacher if they suck dick or take it up the ass. Why the hell people think it's okay to ask a gay dude is beyond me, and honestly, beyond fucking rude.

"C'mon, Danny, wait up," Bo pleaded.

I stopped and waited. This wasn't Bo's fault.

PLAN B | 11

"He's drunk and he's an asshole. Ignore him, man." Bo looked back toward the fire and smiled. "From the way Katie is handing him his ass right now, he won't be bugging us any more tonight. Come back to the fire."

I followed his gaze to see Katie's mouth going a mile a minute and one of her fingers stabbing into Lance's chest. "Pffft. As if I'd let a douchebag like that run me off." I rolled my eyes. "You know me better than that."

"So you'll stay?"

"Not a fucking chance. If I have to watch you and Katie making goo-goo eyes at each other for one more minute, I'll gouge my eyes out. I'm going to head back to the dorm."

Bo looked a little distraught, looking back and forth between Katie and me. Finally his shoulders slumped. "Just let me tell Katie I'm leaving and I'll walk back with ya."

One thing about Bo is he's loyal as hell. He'd be cranky if I agreed, but he'd come with me, blaming himself because I'd gotten upset. Then he'd sit and pout the rest of the night. Yeah, like I wanted to deal with that shit. "Nah, I'm just going to crash anyway. I'm sure you'll have way more fun here. She's a feisty one, that Katie."

Bo briefly glanced back in Katie's direction and smiled. "That she is. You sure?"

"Geeze, papa bear, it's no big deal. I was looking for an excuse to bail." I gave him a shove. "Go on, I'll see you later."

He got.

I cut through the side yard to the sidewalk and headed back toward the dorm. Katie's brother was a total asshole, plain and simple, and kind of creepy with the way he'd seem so fixated on me. The guy's eyes were just—I shuddered and it had nothing to do with the cold. The way Lance had looked at me, the way I'd felt, really did a number on me, and I wrapped my coat tighter around myself. I'm pretty good at reading what people were thinking and feeling, but Lance, I just couldn't quite get a read on. I mean, I'd seen what I thought was disgust, his crass words only intensifying that feeling. I could have sworn it was lust, but I just couldn't be sure, and it bugged me.

By the time I made it back to my room, I'd decided the guy was nothing more than a major jerk without a sliver of manners in that big jock body, but at least meeting Lance hadn't been completely a bad thing. He'd given me an excuse to get out of frat party hell. I'd made up for the ballet, and now it was my turn to pick. A smile curled my lips when I remembered the flyer I'd gotten for an upcoming drag show.

Bo would so totally hate it.

Bo didn't return to the dorm room after the party, but I hadn't expected him to. He'd texted that he and Katie were going to hang with some of Katie's friends and pull an all-nighter. That was fine with me. I was in a shit mood, restless, and I didn't want to hear all the "Katie is so hot, Katie is so awesome, Katie did this, Katie did that." I was happy for Bo, really I was, but Christ, a person could only hear so much about Katie before he fucking lost it.

After showering and scrubbing my face, I crawled into bed, hugged a pillow to my chest, and tried concentrating on the soothing mood music playing through the CD player. It was designed to relax: rushing water, the wind rustling through the trees, birds singing, and melodic pan flutes. It normally worked, but not this time. I tried to focus on the sounds around me, taking slow even breaths in through my nose and out through my mouth. But the harder I tried to relax, the more tense I became.

The thought of the way Lance had looked at me—I'd convinced myself I had in fact seen lust—caused my body to hum. It was creepy and intense. The glint of danger in those gray pools—so, so dangerous—both frightened and excited the hell out of me.

I didn't sleep a wink, just tossed, turned, and tried to get Lance out of my head. But when dawn broke, I was still edgy, my thoughts all jumbled. I spent the entire Saturday trying to stay focused on my lines while in rehearsal for an upcoming production, but the rest of the time, I was pacing the tiny dorm room like a caged animal. I was exhausted, yet too wound up to rest. It was maddening. I couldn't for the life of me figure out what it was about Lance that consumed my thoughts.

CHaPTer
TWO

I HAD an amazing childhood. I grew up in a home full of love with parents who gave me wings and encouraged me to fly in whatever direction I wanted. Both my mom and dad are big into theater and dance and from a young age, I shared their love of flair, playing dress-up, and dance. My mom toured with a ballet troupe for a while until she got pregnant with me and discovered her greatest love was being a stay-at-home mom. And I can honestly say without a hint of hesitation that she was and is the greatest mother on the planet. Devoting her life to me and Dad didn't mean she gave up her love of theater or dance. Instead of being on stage, she had this little person to sit in the audience with—me—and left the public performances to Dad.

In private, however, she and I danced around the house or backyard and put on elaborate plays in the living room for an audience of one. My love for makeup and clothing has nothing to do with me being gay, or at least I don't think it does, and everything to do with my parents passing their love of those things down to me. I don't hide behind the flair. I thrive and feel free within its folds.

When I told my parents I was gay, I was like ten or eleven. I'm not sure why I was so scared to tell them or why I felt my attraction for boys should be a secret, but it did and it ate at me, made me feel like I was a fake. I didn't hide things from them, especially Mom, but somehow this revelation seemed huge.

I remember being nervous, standing there in our kitchen while Mom washed dishes and Dad dried. My secret weighed on me until it felt too heavy, and before I could chicken out, I blurted, "I think I like boys more than girls." Mom turned and smiled at me, handed a dish to Dad, and said, "So do I," and that was that. My sexuality didn't matter to them either way. It didn't define me then and it doesn't now.

I experimented with sex a lot growing up. Even Bo and I did the mutual jerk-off. Boys experiment. At thirteen, you're all about your dick and what it can do and how good it feels when you touch it, and you want to show that shit off. Bo's terminally straight but… well, he's a dude and, like I said, dudes experiment.

Not only did I grow up with loving and accepting parents, but I've also spent a lot of time with people in the arts and entertainment industry. They tend to be—if a bit odd—very accepting of "different," so I've always been very comfortable with who I am. If there was chemistry between me and a guy, then hey, I'm all for fucking, but I don't do relationships. I don't drive myself crazy lusting over straight guys—or any guy. If we hooked up, great. If we didn't, well, I had a more-than-capable hand. I wasn't looking for a relationship. A little physical hookup? Hell yeah! Move in with me, tell me you love me, only me, forever—not a chance. So, why Lance had me all riled up, I didn't have a clue. It was a totally new experience for me.

I don't obsess.

Okay, I do obsess about the theater and my hair. Fine! I also obsess about my makeup and my clothes, but my point is, I don't obsess about men. I wasn't looking for a relationship, I didn't do them. I was all about me, me, me. I put everything I had into my acting career and my future. I would see my name in lights. Broadway or bust, baby! So why I spent an entire weekend consumed with thoughts of Lance Lenard, I was clueless and quite frankly more than a little irritated.

By Sunday, I was just flat-out pissed off when I finally crawled out of bed.

I'd woken suddenly from a dream I couldn't remember, but it didn't take a damn rocket scientist to figure out what it was about. My breathing was labored, my pulse pounded through my veins, and my dick was so flippin' hard it hurt. I shut my eyes and wrapped a hand firmly around it. I'd been so close when I woke, it only took a couple of hard pulls, and I was grunting, groaning, and shooting all over my stomach and chest. It was fast, intense, and felt so goddamn good to let go. As I twitched and jerked through each contraction, I thought finally, finally, the tension in my body would relax. *No.* Sex, jerking off, whatever, is a hell of a stress reliever, except this time the white dots that usually danced behind my eyes when I shot a load were absent, replaced by steel-gray eyes. Now instead of just tense and agitated, I was tense, agitated, wet, and sticky.

Arrogant, rude bastard had insulted me, creeped me out, pissed me off, and made me restless all weekend. Now he was fucking with my orgasms. What the hell was it about the guy? Lance's stare had done something funny to me, and I couldn't quite grasp the meaning. I'd had a few fantasies in high school about straight jock quarterback Trevor McKnight, which had been pretty hot. Maybe that was it, the combination of the lust I'd seen in Lance's eyes bringing back old memories of hot football fantasies.

Thankfully, I woke Monday morning and was finally able to concentrate on something other than Lance. The U-M School of Musical Theater was doing a comedy, *The Boys from Syracuse*, and I'd snagged a starring role. It's based on Shakespeare's *The Comedy of Errors*, set to music. It's considered one of Rodgers and Hart's best musical efforts. Anyway, I got the part of one of the identical twins, Antipholus of Syracuse, who was going around causing all this havoc. I didn't get my mom's grace—I can't dance for shit, two left feet—but I got Dad's voice. I don't think it's as good as his is, but the director thought I was perfect for the part. The show was opening in just under a week. I knew my lines, could do my part and those of the rest of the cast in my sleep. I was ready, all but one thing—I was still debating whether I should dye my hair brown or wear a wig. Plain brown hair is so vapid, and I really, really like the blond and purple—took four and a half hours to get it that way—but wigs, no matter how expensive, just never looked natural on me.

I grabbed a ball cap and my script and quietly slipped out of the dorm. Bo had finally shown up around four that morning looking haggard but happy. There's this little coffee shop just a couple of blocks over called Brewed Awakening that has the best coffee in town. The café was a little fancy, with plenty of gourmet and creative coffee choices, but I like mine with just a little cream and sugar.

The walk over was chilly. I hadn't realized how cold it was and should have grabbed a coat rather than my old black *Kingdom Hearts* hoodie, but it was a short walk and I was too busy thinking about my hair, lines, songs, and Antipholus of Syracuse to be bothered by the weather.

There was hardly anyone in the coffee shop that early—on a college campus, six a.m. is early. I groaned a little to myself when I saw Tiffany behind the counter. It wasn't that I disliked Tiffany. I did like her. But that particular morning I was feeling less than sociable, and if Katie was a chatterbox, Tiffany was the grand dame of talks-way-too-fucking-much. She's slim and tall and—I can't really say beautiful, but maybe cute, in that girl-next-door kind of way. She has dark blonde hair, a crooked smile, and, bless her heart, a major problem with allergies, so she is constantly sniffling. But she's also very, very—and I do mean *very*—friendly.

"Danny!" Tiffany squealed when I stepped up to the counter. "I haven't seen you in like, forever." She then went on and on about how much she'd missed me over the past week and what she'd been up to, as she poured my coffee without needing to ask me what I wanted.

As she added the half-and-half and sugar to my coffee, she talked the entire time. "So, how have you been?"

"Good. And you?"

"How's the play coming along?"

"Great." I reached for my coffee, but she held on to it.

"I bet you're getting excited about opening day, huh?"

"Yup." *Can I please have my coffee now?* I tried taking it again, but she picked it up before I could grab it, and put a sleeve on it.

"Oh. My. God. I was telling a friend of mine how awesome you are, and she's coming with me to see the show."

"That's great. Thank you."

"We've already gotten our tickets," she informed me with a proud smile.

I wasn't usually rude, and I'd chat with her a few minutes, asking her about her classes or her boyfriend, but that morning I really wasn't in the mood for small talk. I threw a couple of bucks on the counter and grabbed my coffee as soon as she released it, and said with a wink, "That's awesome. I'm sure I'll see you both there, but I have to read over my lines. Keep the caffeine coming."

Tiffany got this really happy expression on her face and nodded vigorously. "I will. I will."

Tiffany is very sweet even if a bit infatuated with theater majors. I don't know, I think she somehow thought her pouring coffee in my cup was some kind of important role for the overall success of the show. Hey, if it made her happy and quiet, I was all for telling her she was the most important aspect of my acting career.

I was on my second cup of coffee—trying to concentrate on the script, but I kept getting distracted by thoughts of my hair, wigs, and beauty parlors—when the bell over the door jingled. I glanced over toward the sound and instantly slumped in my chair. I mean, really? What were the chances? I'd been coming to this coffee shop for weeks, always early and never, ever, not once, had I seen him in here.

It was a conspiracy, I tell you.

I pulled my ball cap farther down over my eyes, shifted in my chair so that my back was to him, and prayed like hell he wouldn't notice me.

No such luck.

I waited until he was standing at the counter, his back toward me, then gathered up my script and shoved it into my bag. I was just about to get up and slip through the door when that freaky hair on the back of my neck rising hit me. I looked up and sure as shit, Lance was standing a few feet away from my table, coffee in hand, staring at me. Tiffany obviously didn't know him, because damn, had he gotten a cup of coffee fast. For a second we just stared at each other, and I was doing my best to be all nonchalant and not give away any of the panic I felt. I don't know why I was so freaked out. I mean, yeah, I'd been thinking about him all weekend and how he'd thrilled and creeped me out, but he wasn't looking at me with the same menacing look now. It was more uncertainty, maybe with a little embarrassment thrown in.

"Mind if I join you?"

My first thought was to tell him to piss off, and had he still had that same strange look in his eyes from Friday night or had he just plopped his ass down at my table without asking, I'm sure I would have. But he looked almost timid standing there, and I found myself waving to the chair across from me and saying, "Be my guest."

18 | SJD PeTerson

"Thanks." He took the seat I'd offered, both of his big hands wrapped around his mug, head lowered.

I was all kinds of curious as to why he was here, but he didn't say a word, he just sat there, holding that mug like his life depended on it or some shit. I wasn't about to be the one to start the conversation since he had invited himself; I, in turn, sat there sipping my coffee and waited.

"So," he finally said, but I thought it was a nudge to get me to say something, because that's all he said. I just kept right on drinking my coffee.

We sat in an uncomfortable silence for a few more minutes. I'd set aside the hair-vs.-wig debate for the new should-I-stay-or-should-I-go debate. I was leaning toward going, since it was getting just a little too weird for me. I mean, who the hell invited themselves to join someone and then just sat there staring at their coffee? I was just getting ready to bolt when he finally looked up at me.

"I almost didn't recognize you," he said, meeting my eyes for the first time that morning. "You look different."

Well no shit, Sherlock, I almost responded. *Baseball cap, no makeup, hoodie instead of girly coat—of course I look different, you moron.* Instead, I settled for, "Mmm hmm."

"I was drunk the other night. Not that I'm using that as an excuse, but...." He cleared his throat, his cheeks turning pink. "I'm really sorry for what I said. I mean, I assumed you were gay by the way you were dressed, but it still didn't give me the right to say what I did."

"I am gay."

"But I thought...." He shook his head, a small smile curling his lip. "Okay, I deserved that one."

"Yeah, you did. So are you? Is that why you were asking if I sucked dick?"

Lance's eyes went impossibly wide. "Who, me? Umm... no," he sputtered. "Why, do I look gay to you?"

Actually, I'd seen gay guys who were a hell of a lot more masculine looking than Lance. Big fucking body builders who were total bottoms, chubby bears, twinks who were badass Doms. Hell, I'd met one drag queen who made real women weep with how beautiful and feminine he was, and he was totally straight. Obviously, Lance was

PLAN B | 19

one of those yahoos who believed gay was a lifestyle and all the rest of the stereotypical bullshit. I briefly thought about explaining all this to him, but I realized I didn't really care what Lance thought, and after the weekend I'd spent obsessing over him, I was relieved by that realization.

I downed the last of my lukewarm coffee and then grabbed my bag. "Relax, no one would peg you for gay." Asshole? Yes. Gay? Doubtful. I stood and shouldered my messenger bag. "I gotta run. See you around."

"Did I offend you again?" he asked, jumping to his feet.

"Not really. I need to get to rehearsal." I should have said yes and stormed out, but I knew my mistake the moment his face lit up when I mentioned where I was going.

"Katie mentioned you were a theater major. That's cool."

"Thanks."

"I'm heading that way myself. I'll walk with you."

"Why? I mean, no offense, but why?"

Lance shrugged. "I just figured if your best friend was going to be dating Katie, we might as well get to know each other."

"Katie handed you your ass, did she?" I said with a smirk.

"Uh, yeah. You could say that."

I chuckled as I headed to the door and stepped out, Lance right on my heels. "Well, I'll let you off the hook and tell Bo you apologized and were a perfect gentleman." I turned and offered my hand. "I'm sure you and I won't be running into each other just because my friend is dating your sister. See you around."

Lance took my hand, but instead of shaking it, he held onto it, his gaze heavy on mine. "I'd like to get to know you, regardless," he said. "Plus, I'd like another chance to prove first impressions aren't always true."

I tried to think of something to say, but the way he was looking at me had me all messed up in the head. He said he wasn't gay, but I would have sworn the look in his eyes said he'd eat me up if he had the chance. I really was losing it. Brushing it off to an aftereffect of a confusing and weird weekend—or maybe to being more nervous about the upcoming production than I realized—I pulled my hand free from his and nodded.

As we started walking, Lance attempted to make conversation. "So are you from Michigan?"

"Originally from Royal Oak."

"Katie and I are from Columbiaville, a little-bitty town near Lapeer. Heard of it?"

"No. I've heard of Lapeer though. Never been there, but I know where it is."

"You're not missing anything." He chuckled. "Not much goes on out there but farming and hunting." He scrubbed a hand over his chin. "If you're not doing anything Friday night, why don't you come to the game?"

"What game?"

"Michigan vs. Iowa."

My hands were turning numb from the cold, so I shoved them in the pockets of my hoodie. "Is that football?"

"Uh yeah. You do watch football, don't you?"

I snorted. "No, but obviously you do."

"And play too."

"What position?" Like I really cared, but I was all for anything at this point, even conversation about football, if it gave me an opportunity to figure out what Lance's angle was and why he was being suddenly so friendly.

"Halfback." Lance bumped his shoulder against me, causing me to stumble, but I righted myself quickly before I landed on my ass. Christ, he was strong. "So if you want to go, I can get you a ticket."

His statement had me taken aback. Was he asking me to go or merely offering me free tickets? I shrugged. "Sorry, I can't." I wasn't really sorry. I mean, I was curious as all hell as to why he was offering the tickets, but sitting out in the cold with thousands of crazy people watching men chase around a ball wasn't my idea of an exciting Friday night, even if one of them was Lance. "It's opening night at the theater. I sort of have to be there."

We ran out of conversation after that. As we walked across the campus, I kept my eyes on the sidewalk, but I watched him out of the corner of my eye. Even though he kept glancing at me the entire way, I didn't feel the unease I had the night of the party. And then he stopped and visibly stiffened.

"Hey, I gotta get to practice. Maybe I'll run into you later."

Before I could say anything, he was cutting across me toward two big guys in the distance. After only a few steps, he looked back over his shoulder and said, "I like your other look better." Then he turned and ran.

I was speechless. I just stood there on the sidewalk, the late October wind biting at my cheeks and ears, as I watched Lance race across the lawn. *I like your other look better.* What the fuck! No straight guy ever said they liked a dude in makeup. At least not the kind I had been sporting.

So much for getting Lance out of my head. He was now securely burrowed into the center while I swam in confusion.

Chapter
Three

I DIDN'T see Lance again that week. Between classes, rehearsal, wardrobe nightmares, and wig hunting—I finally gave up and dyed my hair brown—I didn't have time to think about him or the implications behind his last statement to me.

The thing about the theater is if you're going to do it, you give it your all. I can tell you from personal experience there is nothing worse than screwing up in front of a live audience. You feel about two inches high, turn bright red in embarrassment, and you want nothing more than to dig a hole through the wood planks and crawl in it. However, when you get it right, you get a rush like no other, and as the curtain closed on the final show, I was experiencing one hell of a high.

The applause was thunderous, echoing off the walls of the small theater. The roar of the crowd, the screeching whistles only intensified the high. When the curtain opened once again, that sweet feeling ratcheted higher and I was flying as I stared out at the audience. Yes! A frickin' standing ovation! I'd never experienced that thrill, at least not from center stage. My chest was all puffed out and tight, my legs a little wobbly, and my jaw actually ached from how wide my smile was. I took a bow. The show had been a total success. Each night, everyone had been on their game—from lighting, makeup, and wardrobe, actors, to the sound crew—everything just came together and flowed, culminating in the perfect final curtain for *The Boys from Syracuse*.

As I rose, I saw my mom and dad, standing in the second row, and that pressure in my chest grew. Dad was clapping, a huge, proud smile on his face, and Mom was bringing her hands to her mouth, blowing me kisses repeatedly. Bo and Katie were to the right of my mom and they were both applauding, Katie jumping up and down, as they hooted and hollered. I winked and bowed again as the crowd continued to applaud. When I stood once again, my eyes landed on Lance. How I had found him in this huge crowd, I don't know. Luck? Coincidence? Whatever it was, my breath hitched when I saw Lance, his thumb and index finger in his mouth, whistling. He was dressed in a black suit coat with a white T-shirt beneath and ragged jeans. Not exactly the proper attire for the theater, but for the first time it hit me how truly handsome he was. His short hair was spiked; a day or two's worth of dark stubble on his jaw only highlighted his perfectly white smile when he pulled his fingers from his mouth. Jesus, he looked good, and when he winked at me, my knees buckled. I mean fucking buckled and I had to lock them to keep from falling.

I could only stand there and stare at him. A simple gaze, but I felt it like a kiss to my heated flesh. A tingling sensation started at the base of my skull and worked its way down my body, until my toes curled. I wanted him. I'd lusted after guys before, but it was more along the lines of finding them hot and thinking getting up close and personal would be fun, but nothing like I was feeling for Lance. I mean, I really fucking was to the point it was crazy insane how badly I wanted him. Luckily, the curtain closed before I could make a complete fool of myself, and I was able to take a couple of deep breaths when the power he had no longer held me. I tried to calm down enough to get my shaky legs to carry me to the dressing room.

Someone from the cast—I was too dazed to know who—pulled me into a tight hug and slapped me on the back, then another and still another. I shook off the weird feeling that had ignited in me, and flowed with the crowd around me as we all congratulated each other, moving away from the stage together and back toward the dressing area.

Thirty minutes later, I emerged from the "cast only" area dressed in chinos, a dress shirt, tie, and a merino wool Ralph Lauren V-neck pullover vest. I was rocking the preppy look. This wasn't something I normally wore—Granny bought the vest last Christmas—but my parents had plans to take me for a quiet dinner to celebrate before I headed to the cast party. However, I did spend a little extra time teasing and tousling the ugly brown strands of my hair—at least the style was cool. I also added smoky-gray eye makeup, heavy eyeliner, and lip gloss, but I told myself it didn't have anything to do with the possibility that Lance might be in the hall waiting or with the fact that he liked this look.

The first person I spotted was Bo. "Here comes the star of the show now." He was so loud, his voice bellowed over the roar of the crowded hallway.

I rolled my eyes at him. I then spotted my parents standing to his right and Katie to his left. I raised my hand to wave to the group, my motion halting as I swallowed hard and my hand shook a little when I noticed Lance standing next to Katie, his arm draped around the shoulders of some blonde girl I didn't recognize. Was that a friend of his, a girlfriend? To my chagrin, the possibility of the latter bothered the hell out of me. Thankfully, he wasn't looking in my direction, and I turned my attention back toward my parents. I didn't want him to catch me staring at him—those damn gray eyes made me weak—and I sure as shit didn't want to look at the bimbo curled up against his side with her blood-red-clawed hand pressed against his stomach.

I made my way through the crowd; as soon as I was close enough, my mom rushed me and wrapped me in an embrace. "You were so wonderful," she said. I hugged her tight, feeling a swell of pride rippling through me, which only grew in intensity when my dad patted me on the back and hugged us both. He didn't say anything—he didn't need to. The hug and the look in his eyes told me just how proud he was of me.

Bo was the next to congratulate me with a manly knock of his knuckles against mine, followed by a squeal and a brief hug from Katie. For a second, I entertained the idea of grabbing my mom's hand and rushing to the door, but knew it would be rude to ignore Lance. He'd come to watch the show, even waited afterward to see me. The strange feelings I had about him doing crazy things to me were not his fault, but my own scattered brain creating these problems. I manned up and forced myself to look at him. Lance had a wide smile as he extended his hand to me, thankfully using the arm he'd had draped over… ah, who cares? "Awesome show, Danny."

I shook his hand. "Thank you."

That was it, just a handshake and a compliment. No introductions, thank God. What had I been expecting? Better question, what was I dreading? Why hadn't I thought to consider that his girlfriend wanted to come to the show and it had nothing to do with Lance wanting to see me or maybe he just liked the theater? Hadn't he thought the fact that I was a theater major was *cool*? Damn, I was vain, no big surprise there. I had to laugh at myself as I turned back to my parents. I was beginning to think I had a screw loose.

MY PARENTS had reservations at a small restaurant close to the theater, but it seemed everyone else had the same idea. It was standing room only; the noise of several different conversations going on around us made it nearly impossible to chat without screaming. My parents each had one glass of wine, and I settled for a soda with dinner. Damn minimum twenty-one-year-old drinking age law! I could have used a glass of wine to settle the way I still felt, all jittery from seeing Lance. It was nice spending time with them. I knew they missed me and I appreciated the effort, but I was ready for a more relaxed atmosphere. Translation—sweet, nerve calming wine.

By the time I reached the cast party, it was in full swing. I say cast "party" but it was really more of an intimate setting of about thirty people. The group was comprised of a few of us who had become good friends during production or had already built friendships from previously working on other projects, and their close friends or significant others. As usual, the party was held at the home of Lee (who played the sorcerer) and Clifford (who played the tailor's apprentice), both of whom I'd known since the first day of classes during my first semester at U of M. They shared their large Tudor-style house with a couple of other guys who, while big into the theater, hadn't been in *The Boys from Syracuse*. However, they were used to their place being the hot spot for production after-parties.

I found a beer—but since I wasn't in a beer mood, I filled a plastic cup with ginger ale, as the champagne and wine were gone. I knew if I didn't have a cup in my hand, someone would make sure I did. While wine tends to mellow me out, enough beer makes me horny and keeps me pissing every thirty minutes—neither of which I was in the mood to be dealing with that night.

Bo and Katie were sitting on one of the couches in the living room. As soon as I spotted them—and the empty space to Bo's right—I quickened my steps. I plopped my ass down next to Bo, close enough to bump his shoulder, and caused his beer to spill on his lap.

"Hey, asshole!" He wiped at his crotch. "Don't be thinking just because you're a big star or something that I won't kick your ass."

I leaned forward and addressed Katie. "If you haven't figured it out yet, he's totally delusional." I glanced at Bo briefly and wrinkled my nose. "And a major klutz."

"Yeah, I've noticed." She laughed.

"Hey! I'm neither of those things," Bo complained, then scowled when both Katie and I laughed harder.

"Great! Just what my sister needs, another delusional person in her life."

I stiffened and my smile fell as I heard Lance's familiar voice. Turning my head, I found Lance sitting in an overstuffed chair to my right that faced the couch, smiling at me. How had I not seen him when I passed by?

Shocked, all I could do was sit there and gape at him. I had noticed more about him each time we'd run into each other. Like originally, I hadn't thought he was exceptionally attractive, but now I realized it had been the alcohol and his demeanor that had given me that impression. His dark brown hair had sun-streaked highlights; his lips were full and looked very kissable. His smile was slightly crooked, giving him a mischievous expression when he turned it on.

A sharp nudge to my arm from Bo brought me out of my musings. I jerked. "What?" I felt my cheeks heat when I realized I'd been staring at Lance with my mouth open. I snapped it shut. My embarrassment increased, even my ears felt hot, when Lance chuckled as if he'd known what I'd been thinking.

I looked away.

"I hope you don't mind that we invited my brother. His date ditched him."

I shook my head since I didn't yet trust my voice. My throat had gone dry at the same moment my mouth had flopped open.

"She had a long drive back!" Lance protested.

"Uh huh."

"Shut up," he grumbled, but there was no heat behind Lance's words. Obviously just a little friendly sibling banter, but it was enough to take the attention off me and I relaxed a little. I sipped at my soda and said nothing as the two of them went back and forth. Although I kept my head down, eyes glued to the cup in my hand, I was very much aware of Lance and couldn't help but steal glances out of the corner of my eye. It was like I was drawn to him and simply couldn't help myself.

"So what's next?"

It took me a second to realize that the three of them had gone silent and the question was directed at me. I hadn't been paying attention even if I was trying to pretend I was.

"Umm…." I had to clear my throat and try again. "Basically just classes for a while. I got a small part in a show called *August Osage County*, a stand-in part really."

"Are they crazy?" Bo said dramatically. "Putting a star in as a stand-in role?"

"Smartass." I rolled my eyes at Bo and nudged him with my elbow. His beer jostled but he caught it in time. "You're getting better with the reflexes," I teased.

"He's right, you know. You're a lot better than just a stand-in."

My gut got all fluttery when Lance paid me a compliment and I smiled as I replied, "Thank you."

"Hey, how come he doesn't get an elbow to the ribs?" Bo complained, rubbing his hand across his abused side.

"Because he was being sincere. You were just being an ass."

I said that just to irritate Bo and it did. He knew I was kidding, but his eyes began shifting back and forth between Lance and me. Bo knew me too well, and the last thing I needed was for him to notice my attraction to his girlfriend's brother.

Time for a subject change.

"Hey, Katie. How did you do on that ECON test you were stressing over?"

"Won't find out till Tuesday, but pretty sure I did well." She looked up at Bo with a dreamy look in her eyes. "Thanks to Bo. He really came through, helping me study."

I swear to God, she batted her lashes at the man and he turned into a pile of melted goo boy. At that moment, however, I was glad my friend was pussy-whipped, as he forgot all about Lance and me.

I honestly tried to pay attention to what Katie and Bo were saying, but it was hard. I think I did okay, adding a few questions here and there to keep them going, but I was fighting the urge to stare at Lance the entire time. I could feel his eyes on me, and I found it increasingly difficult not to squirm in my seat or keep up with what the lovey couple was saying. I didn't want to know about ECON or tests or classes or anything else to do with school. What I really wanted to know was what Lance was thinking as he stared at me. I really wanted to know if he found me as attractive as I found him, if he'd consider going back to my place and banging the hell out of me.

Sitting there trying to listen to my friends and clamping down on my urge to openly stare was the worst possible time to be thinking about jumping Lance's bones or vice versa, because that line of thinking just made my dick start to swell, and then I didn't dare meet his eyes because I knew he'd see the lust. And wasn't that totally not me. I wasn't shy—when I wanted to know something I asked—but with Lance, he did this crazy shit to me that made me so not... me. I didn't like it, yet I did, and that made no goddamn sense at all.

The longer I sat there trying to figure Lance out, and hoping he'd give me a clue or at least talk to me, the more my tension grew. It was as if someone was wringing my body tighter and tighter as they would a windup toy and my twisty thing was about to pop. I needed to move, to put some space between me and Lance and just fucking breath for a minute. I downed the last of my ginger ale and jumped to my feet.

"I'm going to grab something else to drink. Anyone need anything?"

"I'm good," Bo said without even looking away from Katie, who just shook her head.

"I could use another beer. I'll go with you," Lance offered and started to rise.

"I think I can handle two cups."

My voice was a little strained, which made my reply come out clipped, and it was rude to walk away without looking at him. But I didn't dare. I was already horned up just being around him and I figured it would be better if he thought I was an asshole, rather than thinking I was lusting after him.

I spent a few minutes in the bathroom, fussing with my hair and makeup and giving a good stern talk to my reflection in the mirror. Reminding myself that it had been a very busy week, some strange stuff—like my new obsession with Lance—was happening and I needed to get my shit together and start focusing on the next class and project. It's easier said than done. I was stubborn as hell and finally even my reflection was rolling its eyes at me. But whatever. I did manage to look composed when I emerged, grabbed a soda and a beer, and returned to sit next to Bo all casual-like.

I do love postproduction parties, everyone finally getting to relax and a chance to talk to friends without having to read from a script. The problem with this particular gathering was, between Bo and Katie ignoring me and Lance staring at me, it had become one of the most uncomfortable ones I'd ever attended and that included the *frat* party Bo had forced me to. The adrenaline high from the show was wearing off, and for the first time I realized how weary I was. When I get tired, I get cranky.

I turned toward Lance. He was sitting there drinking his beer, and the blank, creepy expression from the first night I met him had returned to his face. I was relieved that my libido had simmered down, but in its wake was left irritation.

"Do I have something on my face?" I bared my teeth at him. "Anything in my teeth?"

Lance blinked, and then shook his head, like he was trying to clear it. "Uh? What?"

"You keep staring at me. So I must either have something on my face or you are just rude."

"Sorry, I didn't even realize I was." His cheeks flushed. "I zone out when I'm daydreaming."

"It's nighttime, but hey, whatever." I still thought it was rude. I was ready for a hot shower and a lumpy dorm-size bed. I downed my soda and patted Bo's shoulder. "I'm going to head out."

"Wait. What? This is your party," Bo said.

I stood and glared down at my inconsiderate friend. "Between you two lovebirds fawning all over each other, ignoring me and"—I pointed a finger at Lance—"this guy staring at me like I'm some kind of freak with shit in my teeth, I've had all the party fun I can stand for one night. Besides, I'm tired."

"And cranky," Bo muttered.

"Shut up."

Lance stood as well. "Danny, c'mon, man, don't go. I honestly didn't mean to stare."

Katie also got to her feet, her pale cheeks pink. "I didn't mean to be rude, and I promise Lance wasn't trying to be an ass. He's been this weird since he was a kid."

"Gee, thanks a lot," Lance grumbled.

Katie held her hands up. "I didn't mean it like that." She laughed and then said to me, "You think he's staring at you, but in his mind he's not even in the same room. He's the freaky one, but I still love him." She looked up at her brother and stuck her tongue out him playfully.

I was beginning to feel like a drama queen who had just had a little hissy fit and they were all standing around, apologizing and trying to placate me. I could have been up mingling with everyone else. It wasn't their fault I'd been sitting there hoping Lance would say something to me. Nor was it their fault I got pissy when he didn't. Sometimes I could be a true bitch to drama.

When Bo turned to me and said, "We'll go get you a coffee. It'll make you feel better," it only intensified the feeling of being a knob.

I'm sure I would have come up with some wonderfully witty retort like "fuck off" had I not been so worn out. Instead, I just patted his shoulder again and said, "Coffee is the last thing my cranky ass needs. A bed, a pillow, and eight hours hanging with Mr. Sandman is about the only thing that will make me feel better."

"All right. You want me to give you a ride back?"

We were only about four blocks from campus, but Katie lived a few miles away, so Bo had started driving everywhere since he had to pick her up and take her back whenever they did anything together. I was exhausted and briefly thought about taking the offer, but the short walk would do me good. Give me a chance to clear my head.

"Nah, you and Katie go on. I'd rather walk, but thanks." I gave Katie a hug. "Thanks for coming."

"It was my pleasure. You really were amazing on that stage tonight."

I pulled back from the embrace and gave her a small smile. "Thanks."

Bo patted me on the back, but was looking at Lance. "You want to come with?"

He shook his head. "I think I'll walk back with Danny." He glanced at me. "If that's okay?"

"Umm… yeah. Sure." Wow, there went that witty repartee of mine again. I scowled at Lance as he hugged his sister. How in the hell did he do that to me?

Bo and Katie headed out, and after I said my good-byes to Lee, Clifford, and half a dozen other people, Lance and I stepped out the door and headed in the direction of the dorm.

Now that the mystery of the creepy stares was solved, I couldn't help but wonder why Lance was walking along with me. Why wasn't he hanging out with his jock buddies? I really wanted to know what had brought him to the show, and I was very curious as to what he'd been thinking when he was zoned out earlier. Was he thinking about me, obsessing as crazily as I seemed to be?

There goes that vanity of yours again, I thought.

chapter four

MY EARS and nose were numb by the time we made it to the dorm. Neither Lance nor I really said much, both hunched over to block the bitter wind and hurrying to get out of the cold. I was thankful when Lance pushed the door to the entryway open and held it for me; I was too cold to even pull my hands from my pockets. Every muscle in my body was tense and my jaw ached from clenching it so tightly to stop my teeth from chattering. I sighed heavily in relief as a warm blast of air surrounded me as soon as I was inside, and only then did I pull my hands from my pockets and start to vigorously run them up and down my arms.

"Jesus Christ! Talk about blue balls," I complained.

I shoved open the door to the stairs with my shoulder and ran up the flight of stairs to the second floor. I searched my pockets until I found the key to my room as I hurried down the hall. I needed a hot shower, hot cocoa, and a warm bed. Now! I had been so focused on getting out of my cold clothes and into a steamy shower that I forgot about Lance until I opened the door to my room.

"Uh, come on in."

"Thanks. I hope you don't mind." He unbuttoned his coat and shrugged out of it. "I won't stay long, just need to warm up a bit before I head back."

As he cupped his hands together and blew inside them to warm them up, his eyes scanned the small room and he obviously was able to tell which side belonged to whom. It wasn't that difficult. Bo had the boring nondecorated side. Ugly plain-brown bedspread, desk perfectly organized and uncluttered. Not a single poster or picture on the wall above his bed. Mine? My side was frickin' awesome. Theater masks, bright boas in pink, purple, and yellow, collage of photos of my different performances. And if that wasn't a dead giveaway, the makeshift desk/vanity covered with makeup, hair supplies, and jewelry certainly was. Lance sat on Bo's bed, set his coat next to him, and ran his hands along his thighs.

I pulled off my own coat and threw it on my bed. "What do you mean, before you head back?" I asked and flipped on the little space heater I kept next to my bed.

"I left my car back at the party."

"Why the hell did you do that? It's frickin' cold out. Or didn't you notice?"

"You said you wanted to walk." He shrugged and picked at a loose thread on his jeans.

I just stood and studied him, trying to figure out if he was for real. He barely knew me and yet he'd shown up to my show, came to the party even after his date bailed on him, and now he'd walked me across campus in freezing temperatures when he had a car? He either really liked me or the guy was totally wacked.

"What? I just wanted to make sure you made it back okay."

I sat back on my bed, forearms resting on my knees, and stared at the floor, letting his statement sink in. I couldn't, for the life of me, figure this guy out. I looked up at him. "I haven't decided if you are a nice guy or a total fucking weirdo."

Lance's lip curled into a slight smile. "A little of both, I guess."

"Uh yeah. That makes me feel a whole lot better."

"Oh, like you're not a little weird. I mean, dude, you're wearing fake eyelashes."

Okay, he had me there. "Point taken." I batted said eyelashes at him, which made his smile grow. I liked his smile—his whole face lit up with its appearance. "But at least I'm not the one who zones out and gets all freaky while daydreaming." I gave him a poignant look. "Care to share what made you freaky?"

Lance shook his head, his chilled cheeks going a deeper shade of red. "Just stuff."

Oh, damn, was he cute when he blushed. And now that I didn't have to try and pretend I wasn't looking at him, I started to feel a little more at ease, enough to want to tease him. "Naughty stuff?" I prodded.

"Just stuff," he repeated, suddenly very interested in my wall décor. "Those are great pictures," he said pointing toward the collage. Now I was really intrigued, but it didn't appear I'd be getting much more on the subject out of him, at least not at the moment, and I wanted a hot shower more than I wanted to push him. But we *would* be coming back to this subject in the very near future. I stood and went to the closet. "I need a hot shower," I said as I grabbed some sweats and a T-shirt as well as my toiletry bag from the shelf.

When I stepped out of the closet, Lance had kicked off his shoes and was now sprawled out on the bed, propped up on pillows with his hands behind his head, a study of someone totally laid-back. I arched my brows at him. "Make yourself at home."

"Cool." He nodded toward the flat screen Bo had attached to the wall. Lord knows the man had to have something decent to watch his *Star Trek* twenty-four-volume box set on. "Mind if I watch some TV while you're gone?"

"Help yourself. The remote's in the top drawer of the desk." I pointed at Bo's desk and grabbed my towel from its hook. "I'll be right back."

Lance didn't respond, just rolled over, pulled open the drawer, and grabbed the remote. I wasn't sure how I felt about leaving him in my room alone. What if he started digging through my stuff? Found my naughty box, the giant dildo? I groaned silently at the thought. I knew I should have thrown that damn thing away. No, I am not a size queen; it was a joke, a big dick award from Lee after one of my performances. The last first impression you want to give someone is that you're into dicks the size of a man's forearm, but…. I glanced at the reclining Lance then to the closet where I'd hidden the box. Torn. I really wanted a shower, and the way he'd stretched out on Bo's bed, it looked as if he was making himself comfortable for the night. *Screw it*. I rushed out of the room and hurried down the hall. The sooner I got my shower, the sooner I'd be able to get back and figure out Lance's angle. I admit I was very much intrigued.

When I returned to my room, damp but minus the cold ache that had settled into me earlier, thankfully, Lance was still in his comfy position and didn't look as if he'd moved. I cringed as I heard "Beam me up, Scotty" blaring from the flat screen. Great, another Trekkie. "Please don't tell me you like this shit?" I asked while running the towel over my wet hair.

Lance didn't immediately respond. His eyes wandered down my body, that mischievous grin of his curling his top lip as his eyes roamed, and I shuddered. When his eyes finally met mine, my breath hitched at how dark his eyes had turned. Had they really darkened with lust or was it my vanity and ego making me see things that weren't there? Not sure about the answer to that, but sadly I think it was the latter.

"Nope, it was already set up to play. By the way, your cell phone was chirping."

"Thanks." I hung up my towel and rummaged in my coat pocket until I found my cell, trying my best not to show how he had affected me. I flipped open my phone. A text from Bo read: *Don't wait up. See you tomorrow.*

"Bo's not coming back tonight, is he?"

I spun around and glared at Lance. "You so did not check my phone."

He held his hands up, like he was ready to defend against attack. "Hell no! I got a text from Katie letting me know she and Bo were pulling an"—he made the sign for quotation marks with his fingers— "all-night study session. Didn't realize that was what they called it these days." He chuckled.

Relieved that Lance hadn't been snooping, or at least I didn't feel as if he had, I set my cell on the vanity, crawled up on my bed, and sat Indian-style with my back against the wall, facing him. "So what's your story?" I asked, not wasting any time in satisfying my curiosity. Lance still made me all, I don't know, weird, but in my own room, I felt a little bit more in control of myself.

He hit the Mute button on the remote and rolled over onto his side, cheek resting against his palm, propping his head up. "Whatcha mean?"

"Was it your idea to come to the show tonight or your date's?"

"Mine."

I cocked my head at him. "You ever been to a musical before tonight?"

"No."

"Not even in high school? Maybe junior high?"

He shook his head slightly. "No. Why?"

I crossed my arms over my chest. "So why the sudden interest in musicals? Better question, why the sudden interest in the faggot friend of your sister's boyfriend?"

He pursed his lips, gaze turning cold. "I don't like that word."

"Which one, musical or faggot?"

Lance narrowed his eyes as if I'd offended him but didn't respond.

"Oh, come on. Don't tell me you and your jock friends don't use that description all the time. Its use, I'm sure, is in the Macho Jock handbook and mandatory for club members."

Yeah, I was being a mean little prick, but really? I knew how guys acted when they all got together, and seeing Lance act like he was the one offended by the derogatory slur just sort of irritated the hell out of me. Actually, I think it wasn't just his reaction to my word choice but also the uncertainty and confusion I'd been feeling that was finally getting to me. It just rather bubbled up to the surface at that moment. Straight dudes do not suddenly start liking musicals and following around gay dudes for no reason. I didn't believe his story about wanting to get to know me because of Katie and Bo, and if he wasn't gay, was he setting me up for some kind of prank? Perhaps a bashing?

Lance sat up, feet on the floor, and glared at me. "Well, I don't," he said adamantly. "Why are you acting like such an asshole?"

I glared right back. "Why are you here?"

Lance's shoulders slumped and he looked down at the floor. "I told you, I just—"

"Cut the bullshit. There is more to it than just wanting to get to know me because your sister is dating my friend, and if there isn't, that's some scary mafia kind of shit. You plan to make me an offer I can't refuse? Horse head in my bed if I don't keep my friend in line?"

Lance chuckled at that and lifted his head. "Uh, no."

"That's a relief. So…."

Lance flopped back on the bed, shifting until he was in the same position as before, head propped up on his hand. "You telling me there's some reason I shouldn't want to get to know you?"

"Please! I'm fabulous. But in my experience, straight jocks aren't usually smart enough to figure that out." I ruffled my damp hair as I rolled my eyes. "Must be all those muscles taking up the necessary blood the brain needs."

"Hey! Not all jocks are like that."

"Oh, really? How many of your football buddies would be seen with me?"

"Well." Lance's brow creased. "I don't know them all, but I'm sure some of them would."

"Do you know any, personally?" I pressed.

"I don't know, I haven't asked them."

"Mmm hmm."

"What?" Lance shifted appearing to be uncomfortable with the line of questioning.

"I'm just saying that, in my experience, most jocks aren't secure enough with their masculinity to be seen with a gay guy. Heaven forbid someone think them gay." I shrugged. "I just think it's pretty stupid."

"Yeah, I guess that's true." Lance seemed to relax a little.

The silence stretched out and as I sat there watching him I realized he hadn't actually answered my question of why he was here. Why he had gone out of his way to walk me home, unless…. "Have you ever been with a guy, Lance?"

"No!"

"Ever thought about it or fantasized about being with a guy?"

Lance's brow furrowed ever so slightly. "No."

Lance had been quick with his answer when I'd asked him if he'd been with a guy, but I knew he was lying about not thinking about it by the way he'd hesitated. "Bullshit. Not even when you were younger?"

"You always this bold?"

A shiver ran through me as the heat from the shower had worn off. I pulled the covers back and slid beneath them, lying on my side, one hand beneath my pillow, before I answered. "Pretty much. I don't believe in beating around the bush. So have you?"

He didn't seem to be in any hurry to answer my question, if at all. I was interested in what Lance was hiding, but now that I was warm and stretched out in my bed, the weariness I'd felt earlier came back in a rush. My eyes were suddenly heavy and I had to struggle to keep them open.

"Once," he said quietly.

My eyes flew open wide. I hadn't expected that. Well, I had suspected that he'd been at least attracted to a man before, but I hadn't thought he'd admit it. "Do tell."

Lance's expression was neutral, but he couldn't hide the color that had infused his cheeks. "Some buddies of mine took me to a strip club up in Canada for my nineteenth birthday."

"You went to a strip club, like with naked chicks dancing all around, and you were checking out the guys? Dude, you are so gay." Lance shot me a dirty look, and I had to bury my head under the pillow to muffle my laughter until I could get myself under control.

"Fuck you. It was one of the dancers I got all hot and bothered about, thank you very much."

"Sorry." Another snort of laughter escaped me and I covered my mouth with my hand.

"She had the most amazing legs and ass I'd ever seen." He rolled onto his back, hands held out from his chest as if they were cupping boobs. "And the most amazing set of knockers."

"I get the picture. So what does your trip to a strip club and falling for one of the dancers have to do with my question?"

"I'm getting to it." Lance stared up at the ceiling while he spoke, like he was remembering it. "The whole night was, like, surreal. Here I was in a club, drinking legally for the first time, thinking I'm all badass, ya know?"

"Mmm hmm." The heat in the room only added to my comfort and I snuggled further into my bed.

"So we're watching these girls pole dancing and I'm drinking like a fish. Then my friends, they get this chick whose mini jean skirt I've been stuffing money into all night to give me a lap dance. I was fucking intimidated as hell, I'm not really an exhibitionist, but I was not about to say no. Here I was this kid and this hot chick was rubbing all over me right there in front of everyone."

I pulled the covers up around me tighter. Lance's story with him and some chick wasn't really what I wanted to hear about. I was warm and snuggly and my pillow was cradling my head just right, muscles completely relaxed, and I was beginning to drift off again.

"I don't know if it was the rush of the crowd, her, the beer I'd consumed, or just the fact that I was a horny little son of a bitch and my buddies were egging me on, but I got real bold. I knew the rules: everyone had warned me not to touch the girls. They have signs posted and everything. But I wasn't thinking about the rules or that I might get kicked out of the club. I was all horned up and emboldened by the hoots and hollers of my buddies, and I grabbed her by the hips and pulled her down on me, right there in front of everyone, like she was riding me." Lance turned his head to look at me. "I got so fucking turned on."

"You know what," I said, then yawned. "Glad you had such a great time with your birthday stripper. I don't mean to be rude, but I'm exhausted. Do you mind locking the door on your way out?" My eyes had become so heavy I gave up trying to keep them open. It was useless.

"I thought you were curious about my first time being attracted to a guy?"

"I was, but it was a simple yes or no question. Nothing against big-boobed strippers, but they really don't do much for me, nor you getting hard for one, for that matter." My words were slurred and I'd already started to fall over the edge into sleep, so I'm not sure of my exact statement.

I heard the TV click off and, from behind my closed eyes, saw the light on Bo's desk go out. I think he may have said something else, but I can't be sure. It was lost on me as I fell into blackness. Looking back, I suppose I should have been concerned that I had fallen asleep with a practical stranger in my room, but I was just too tired to really care about it at that moment. Besides, both Katie and Bo had known Lance was walking me back to the room. If there had been any real danger to me, I'd like to have thought they would have said something.

CHAPTER
FIVE

I WAS in that strange place between sleep and wakefulness. A place that seems both real and dreamlike and they merge until you're not sure which one is reality. It was in that state that I could have sworn I felt Lance standing above me, staring at me, and then the sensation was gone, replaced by nothingness. Fingers gently brushed my long bangs from my forehead, the touch like a whisper, just barely there. Soft lips pressed gently against mine. Somewhere within me, I knew I wanted this kiss, more than anything, wanted it to deepen. To lose myself, explore its warmth with tongue, but before I could open to it, the lips were gone and I drifted back into the blackness of sleep.

The click of the door closing brought me out of my light sleep. I groaned and squeezed my eyes shut at the harsh light, pulled the covers up over my head, and buried my face in my pillow. "Christ, Bo! Do you need every light on in the room?"

"Sorry."

I jerked to a sitting position, blinking rapidly to adjust to the harsh overhead florescent light, and gaped when Lance's familiar form came into focus. He was standing near the door, a tray with two coffees in one hand and a brown bag in the other.

"I got muffins and coffee." He walked farther into the room and set them down on Bo's desk. "Wasn't sure what you wanted in your coffee but I grabbed a bunch of cream and sugar."

I closed my eyes and shook my head. When I opened them again, he was still standing there, but now he was staring at me. "I take it you're not much of a morning person?" He chuckled.

"Uh...." I swallowed past my dry throat and ran a hand through my tangled hair. "Not really. What the hell are you doing here?"

"I told you, bringing you breakfast. What do you want in your coffee?"

"Black is fine." I normally took a little cream and sugar, but I figured I needed the bitter taste of pure rotgut coffee to snap me out of my stupor.

Was I still dreaming? I pulled the covers up further on my lap and discreetly pinched my thigh. *Ow*. Nope, I wasn't dreaming.

Lance held out a Styrofoam cup for me that I gratefully accepted. "Thanks."

He nodded then added several packets of sugar and cream to the other coffee before taking it and sitting on the edge of Bo's bed. I watched him as he blew on the steaming brew before taking a small sip. I did the same with mine, needing the caffeine desperately. The strange dreamlike events from the night before, then waking to find Lance in my room—and with breakfast no less—had me a little frazzled. I'm not a morning person, never have been, but this particular morning I was struggling even more than normal to throw off the effects of sleep.

"What time do you have class?"

I glanced at the digital clock next to my bed—*7:05 AM*—and groaned. I gave him an annoyed look. "Not until ten."

"Cool. I don't have class until eleven. We can spend the morning together if you like." He set his coffee down, grabbed the brown bag, and pulled out a muffin. "Blueberry?"

"No."

"I've got chocolate chip, banana nut, and apple cinnamon."

I wanted to stay annoyed at Lance, maybe even throw a good temper tantrum since I hated to be woken up early, but my irritation couldn't stand against the hopeful smile on Lance's face. And, he did have breakfast.

"Chocolate chip," I said and held out my hand.

Lance's smile grew even wider. He rummaged in the bag, handed me a muffin, and dug into his. "So what do you want to do this morning?"

I took a bite from my muffin, the chocolaty flavor delicious, and the rest of my irritation drained away. "I don't know." After another bite, I washed it down with coffee before continuing. "Not really time to do much. What about later today?"

Lance stuffed the rest of his muffin in his mouth. "Can't. I have a class at three then practice right after," he said, although it was a little hard to understand him, since his mouth was so full. He grabbed another muffin out of the bag and peeled off the paper.

To my shock, he shoved half of the muffin in his mouth. "How about a class on manners," I said against the rim of my cup.

"What was that?"

My sleep-addled brain finally came back online and I realized I was sitting in my dorm at seven in the morning having breakfast with Lance. Talk about fucking slow! "Did you stay here all night?"

Lance nodded and wiped a hand across his mouth. "Yeah, sorry about that. I was only going to rest my eyes before I headed back to get my car. Guess I fell asleep."

The memories of Lance standing over me, his touch…. I brought my hand to my mouth and touched my lips as the kiss flashed in my head. They were only dreams—or were they? I still wasn't sure, but I was beginning to lean more toward the side of reality. I wasn't going to ask him, just in case, but damn, the memories of it, whether real or not, made my stomach flutter.

"You okay?"

"I'm fine. Just not enough coffee yet." I took another gulp.

"You really aren't a morning person, are you?"

I shook my head.

"Would you rather meet for lunch than do something now? I have time between my first and second class."

I'd always been one of those gabby kind of people. Hadn't ever been bested in wit or sarcasm, but something about Lance, from the first time I'd met him, left me speechless most of the time. So instead of sounding too eager and telling him I'd call him, take a number, or I was having lunch with some hot stud, I just said, "Yes."

"Cool!"

Lance downed the last of his coffee and threw the cup into the small wastebasket under the desk. He then stuffed his half-eaten muffin back into the bag and stood. "Say, twelve fifteen at the deli?"

Again my wit shone and I responded with, "Yes." Damn, I was on a roll.

The speechlessness and off-kilter shit just heightened when he moved close and leaned over me. My breath caught as I stared back at those stunning eyes and heat infused my groin. I could feel his warm breath against my mouth, practically taste the mix of blueberry, banana, and coffee. I moved my cup to my lap, hoping to hide my growing arousal as he continued to stare at me. Neither of us said a word and a voice in my head started screaming, *kiss me, touch me, anything*, but he did no such thing.

"Do you remember our conversation last night?"

"Which part?" I asked, my voice a little breathy.

"The part where you asked me about whether or not I'd ever been attracted to a guy?"

Lance being so close, feeling his heat, I could only nod. I didn't trust my voice.

"And how turned on I got from the lap dance my buddies got for me?"

Again, I could only nod. My cock had gone from pleasantly aroused to throbbing, and I pressed the bottom of my cup against it to keep the linens from tenting.

He was silent for long moments. His eyes wandered from my face to my rapidly rising and falling chest then down farther, and I hoped the Styrofoam and cotton barrier was enough to hide how he was affecting me. I don't know what he was searching for, or maybe he was building up some courage to say what he was thinking, but whatever it was, he must have found it. He leaned in closer still until I felt his sweet breath against my neck, just below my ear, and I shuddered with the tingling sensation.

"That stripper ground against me." He pressed a kiss to the side of my neck and I had to stifle a moan. A moan that caught in my throat when he said, "His dick was nearly as hard as my own."

I sat there, mouth open wide, shaft throbbing, as Lance straightened and walked to the door. Without a backward glance, he opened the door and stepped out. I heard his deep rumbling chuckle as he closed the door behind him. Bastard somehow knew exactly how that revelation would affect me.

I don't know how long I sat there staring at that closed door because it wasn't wood and metal I was seeing. An image of Lance gripping that stripper's hips, rubbing their cocks against one another, played through my mind until I was on the verge of coming, and I hadn't even touched myself.

It explained so much. The heated looks he'd given me, why he'd been going out of his way to get to know me, why he'd kissed me while I slept.

"Oh, fuck!"

The memory of those soft lips against mine combined with the images in my head and I set the cup I'd been gripping on the desk. My heart was hammering in my chest as I shoved the covers and my sweats down and wrapped my fist around my cock. I stroked my entire length from base to tip, teasing at the flared head with my thumb before moving back down. Behind my closed eyes, I could envision Lance thrusting up out of his chair, denim-encased cock rubbing against the stripper's silk-covered prick. My cock swelled further when the stripper morphed and it was me who was giving Lance a lap dance, rubbing my prick against his as his big hands held my hips in a bruising grip.

His scent was still strong in the air and the flesh below my ear still tingled from his warm lips as I continued to pleasure myself. It didn't take long, hips working, pushing my pulsing cock into my tight fist, and I had to bite down on my lip to keep from shouting out my pleasure as I came.

Then I began to laugh. The whole story of Lance and the stripper was just frickin' hilarious to me. Even more gut-busting was putting myself in that stripper's high-heeled shoes and giving him a lap dance. That would not have been jerk-worthy, not with my two left feet.

I DON'T, nor have I ever, thought of myself as a drag queen. Never wanted to be. Not that I have anything against those who do, I just never really thought of trying to intentionally pass myself off as a woman. I loved painting my eyes and lips, had enough hair products, straighteners, styling tools, and barrettes to make most girls green with envy. Still, I never tried to "hide" the fact that I was a man. I got off on the curious looks I'd get as someone tried to figure out what I was. I've always hated labels, and I was just as likely to shop at Victoria's Secret—love their Pink line—as American Outfitters. I called my style… me. If I liked it, I wore it—there was no rhyme or reason.

However, before meeting Lance for lunch, I spent extra time in front of the mirror and added a few more "feminine" touches than normal. I'd also chosen a pair of black silk skinny pants with matching knee-high boots sporting six-inch heels, a pale yellow blouse with white, black, and yellow swirl designs, and a fringed scarf tied around my neck. Because of the freezing temps, I added a calf-length black wool coat, a yellow knit beret, and yellow fluffy mittens. I admit I was very, very feminine in appearance but I had decided after Lance had left my dorm that I was going to be that gay-curious man's first, come hell or high water. I pulled out the big guns.

Some of my jolly mood in anticipation of seeing Lance fell as I rounded the corner and saw the line outside the deli. It was one of the most popular places to eat. Not only was the food cheap, it tasted good and was right on campus. Shit! I only had an hour before my next class and I was hungry. The half muffin I'd had earlier hadn't been enough.

As I walked past the window, I scanned through the crowd inside, hoping Lance had gotten there early and had a table. No such luck. He wasn't sitting at any of the tables, at the counter, and from what I could tell, he wasn't among the crowd waiting in line either. I sighed and rubbed my hands together. I could already feel the cold wind seeping through the knitted mittens.

After about five minutes, I started shifting my weight from side to side. My footwear wasn't exactly winter-friendly and my toes were starting to go as numb as my ears and nose. I did my best to cover my face with my mittens to block the wind. Rudolph was not a good look for me. I still hadn't spotted Lance and was seriously contemplating heading back to the dorm, when a car horn sounded, grabbing my attention.

An older red Chevy, I think it was a Cavalier, had pulled to a stop. The passenger side window went down slowly, and I spotted Lance leaning across the seat. "Danny, c'mon, get in."

He didn't have to ask me twice. I'd already left my place in line and was heading for the car. Just as I got to it, the door was pushed open and I slid into the seat and slammed the door.

"Oh, thank God you showed up when you did. I was seriously debating whether another few minutes of waiting were worth freezing my nuts off."

Lance chuckled and pulled away from the road. "Wouldn't want that to happen."

"Yeah, no shit," I agreed, rolling up the window. Only then did I notice the smell of pizza sauce, sausage, and yeast. "You got pizza?"

"Yeah, I left class early thinking I'd be able to get a table." He shrugged and turned on his blinker. "Guess everyone had that same idea. It was packed by eleven thirty, so I went and grabbed us a pizza." He turned right at the next intersection.

"Nice recovery. I'm starving."

Lance winked at me. "Then you'll be glad to know I got a large."

"This is where you're taking me to lunch?" I questioned, as he pulled into the parking garage.

"Impressed, aren't you?"

I gave him my best exasperated look and rolled my eyes. "Totally."

"I knew you would be."

Actually, I was impressed. I only had about fifty minutes before I had to be back in class and his thoughtfulness meant I wasn't going to have to wait in line anywhere, or worse, go hungry for the next couple of hours.

He pulled into a deserted section of the garage and parked. He kept the car running, the heater on full blast, reached behind him, grabbed the pizza box, and opened it. I pulled off my mittens and grabbed a slice. "Thanks."

"You're welcome."

We ate in silence for a couple of minutes. Lance's table manners were not much better than at breakfast, and he shoved two slices into his mouth for each slice I ate. He'd also gotten us each a Coke and I washed down the last of my lunch before turning in my seat and facing him.

"Okay, so I take it back."

"Take what back?"

"Not all jocks are meatheads. Lunch was great. What do I owe you?"

"Nothing. My treat."

"I can't—"

He waved me off. "I invited you. You can always get lunch next time." He waggled his brows at me. "Or dinner."

"Next time, huh?" I laughed. "Who said there would be a next time?"

"Well a guy can hope, can't he?"

He turned in his seat to face me, back leaning against his door, as his eyes wandered from my face down my open coat to my lap. Each time we were together, Lance seemed to become a little bolder, like he was having the same difficulty I was hiding the attraction. When he reached my heeled boots, he licked his lips and his eyes were dark with desire—they really were dark this time and not just my vanity coloring them—when they once again met mine. "You look great."

"For a guy who claims he's never been with another guy, you sure seem comfortable checking one out."

He shrugged.

"How old are you?"

He wasn't expecting that question after his admission, as evidenced by the way he cocked his head and hesitated slightly. "Twenty-one. Why?"

"And you were nineteen when your buddies took you to the strip club?"

"Yes."

"And in two years you've never once acted on your curiosity?"

He shook his head. "I…." He swallowed and shifted slightly in his seat. "I thought about it a couple of times. Even went to a gay club once."

"And?"

"I didn't go in. Just stood outside watching all these guys going in, hugging each other, kissing and…." He shifted nervously again. "It just didn't feel right. After that, I started talking to this dude on the

Internet and thought about hooking up with him. Went as far as to chat on the phone and set up a date, but I chickened out at the last minute."

"Why do I have a hard time believing that?"

"I'm serious. It's not like I know a lot of gay guys or get the chance to meet them between school, football, friends, and my family. Besides, I haven't really been attracted to anyone like I was that stripper. Well, not until now."

I wasn't sure if I was flattered or pissed off at his admission. Did it mean he was actually attracted to women and thought I looked like a woman? It was my turn to shift in my seat. His eyes were heavy on me, my pulse increasing. My breath must have increased too, since the windows in the car were fogged up. I wanted him, so did I really care how he saw me? Hadn't I intentionally added a more feminine touch to attract him?

"I'm going to assume since you keep showing up, I'm the 'until now'?"

He didn't answer, but he didn't have to. I saw the answer in his eyes as he shifted and leaned across the car. I found myself meeting him halfway. The first press of lips was hesitant, cautious. It was as if he wasn't sure he should be doing this, but then he licked at my bottom lip and the second I opened my mouth, all the hesitancy was gone. His hand went to the back of my head and pulled me toward him as his tongue plunged deep. A husky moan rumbled up out of him as I opened wide and let him explore and take the kiss where he needed it to go.

Lance had started out reluctant, but as the kiss went on, he became more aggressive, demanding. His hand tightened in my hair and forced my head to the side, and he continued to dominate my mouth. The clash of lips, teeth, and tongue was all-consuming, my toes curling, and shaft hardening in response.

I placed my hands on his shoulders, my fingers digging into the bulging muscles. Without warning, Lance released his hold on me and jerked back, eyes wide and wild as he stared at me. A strange expression crossed his face, one I couldn't quite identify as I fought to get air back in my lungs.

"I shouldn't be…." Lance sat back in his seat, eyes forward. His hand shook when he reached out and adjusted the flow of the heater so it was now blowing directly on the fogged-up windshield. "I gotta get to class."

"You shouldn't be what?"

He scrubbed his hands over his face, big chest heaving, looking all kinds of panicked.

What the hell? I knew he had been into the kiss. I had felt its intensity in every cell of my being. He pulled his coat around him, covered his lap, but not before I saw how hard he was. As I continued to stare at him, trying to figure out what had caused the sudden shift, he crossed one arm across his body, his hand going to his shoulder. He continued to stare at the defrosting window and rubbed at the spot where I had gripped him.

He continued to rub at the spot, a peculiar look on his face. I sat there watching him and I wanted to be pissed. The selfish part of me was in fact pretty riled. I hadn't wanted the kiss to end. I wanted it to be the beginning of hot and horny fun. But the other part of me, the part that wasn't quite so shallow, felt bad for Lance. The kiss had gone from hesitant to hot, growing in intensity until it had a sharp edge. I couldn't help but think that on some level, Lance had known he was kissing a man, could tell how strong and raw it became as he began releasing the reins he kept on that powerful body. However, when he felt the strength in my grip, the other side of Lance, the part that society had created, came to the surface reminding him that what he was doing was wrong. It wasn't that I could read his mind, but his statement "I shouldn't be" was telling, and I was damn sure as I watched him struggle that the rest of the statement would have been *doing this*, if he'd continued. I shifted in my own seat and pulled the seat belt across me, fastening it. I hid the large bulge I was sporting beneath my coat. Lance was freaked out enough at the moment without me adding to it.

"Same here. If you'll just drop me back off at the deli, I can walk from there."

The sound of my voice must have jolted him from his thoughts, because he jumped then put the car in gear. "I can drop you off at your next class."

I hid my disappointment and worked to keep my voice neutral. "If you could drop me off at the music library, I'd appreciate it."

"Sure."

The silence in the car was thick and uncomfortable as we made our way across campus. The only sound was the rush of the heater and the steady swoosh of the windshield wipers. The sky had opened up while we'd been in the parking garage, and the snow fell heavily in large white flakes. Winter had come early.

I stared out my window, watching the flakes as they swirled in the air, my thoughts consumed with what had just taken place between us. Lance had been the initiator of both kisses—yes, both kisses, as I was sure the kiss I had experienced the night before was real—yet I had the distinct feeling that I would have to be the aggressor if anything beyond kissing was to happen. I liked the dance between men. Feeling each other out, figuring out their preferences without coming outright and asking. I already knew Lance was curious, but exactly how far he was willing to go to satisfy his curiosity, I didn't have a clue. I was also dying to know what was going on in his head, but I had no idea how to ask him. It wasn't like I had a lot of experience with closeted guys. I just didn't think *So that first male-on-male kiss really freaked you out, huh?* was the proper postkiss etiquette.

Lance dropped me off at the library, and as I climbed out, he called out my name at the last minute. I turned around to find him staring at me, his mouth partially open, and then he seemed to think better of what he was going to say, snapped it closed, and turned back to look out the front of the car, both hands gripping the steering wheel. "See you later," was all he said.

"See ya." I shut the door and he pulled away.

I was just stepping into the library when my cell phone chirped. I pulled off my mitten and flipped it open. I didn't recognize the number but I knew who it was from the text.

Can I see you after practice?

Oh yeah! Definitely interested, which meant I still had a shot at hot and horny fun. I'd just have to take it slow, was all. I smiled and stuck my phone back in my pocket without responding.

CHaPTer
SIX

I IGNORED Lance's text on Monday, the two on Tuesday, as well as the multiple texts on Wednesday. I also had been particularly cranky, and not once in those three days had I shaved, worn anything that could be considered the least bit girlish, and I hadn't applied so much as lip gloss. By Thursday morning, Bo was checking my forehead for signs of a temperature.

"Dude, I know you're sick. You sure you don't want me to cut class and take you to the clinic?"

"Shut up." I scratched at the stubble on my jaw.

Christ, it itched. I was going to do some serious damage to my face if I wasn't careful. As far as I'd fallen into macho mode, I hadn't fallen so far that I hadn't kept up my nails. Okay, I admit I'd also gone for a pedicure that week, but dammit, I needed some kind of pampering. I kept expecting Lance to show up, but as of yet he hadn't, and my resolve was quickly crumbling.

"How many this morning?"

"None of your business."

Lance had texted me twice, but I'd gotten smart and put my phone on silent any time Bo was around.

"Are you ever going to tell me what you two are fighting about?"

"We're not fighting!"

"Lance keeps telling Katie the same thing. Do you have the hots for him?"

"Hell no," I lied. "When have you ever known me to chase after straight guys? Men chase me, not the other way around."

"From the amount of texts you're getting, I'd say he was chasing you pretty hard. Which, come to think of it, is pretty weird."

"You ever think it's you he's trying to keep tabs on?"

Bo slipped his coat on and moved to stand near the door. "What?" he said, hand on the doorknob. "Why the hell would he keep tabs on me?"

"You are dating his sister and he seems a little possessive."

Bo paled. "You really think—"

"Yeah, I do. I know I'd be a little concerned if you were dating mine. I'd want to keep an eye on you."

I obviously didn't do a good job of hiding my amusement when Bo's eyes narrowed and he walked out, flipping me off over his shoulder before he slammed the door shut.

God, he was so easy to sidetrack.

I scratched at my jaw again, the insistent itch driving me out of my head, and for what? Lance apparently wasn't going to show up to find out why I wasn't answering his texts. I admit I was acting a little high schoolish, but I guess I wanted to know how far he'd go to see me again. When he hadn't come by on the third day, I'd told myself I didn't care and wasn't even sure I liked the son of a bitch beyond his physical attributes, so why should I care if he saw me as a man or a woman? To make matters worse, I looked like shit.

Two hours later, I was sitting in a comfortable leather chair, black cape draped over me, staring at my hideous reflection in a large mirror. "Carlos, give me the works."

I wasn't surprised when later that night—my hair once again a sexy blond color with black/blue streaks, total makeover including eyebrows waxed and facial, the damned stubble gone—that there was a knock at the door. I considered not answering, but the pounding was insistent, getting louder by the second and when Lance bellowed, "Danny, I know you're in there!" I scrambled off the bed and jerked the door open.

Lance stood on the other side of the door, face red, nostrils flaring. He was dressed in a gray pullover hoodie, faded jeans, and dammit did he look good with his aggressive demeanor and flushed face.

"What the hell do you want?"

"Why haven't you been answering my text messages?"

He crowded me, pushed me back from the door, and closed it behind him. His eyes scanned the small space over my shoulder; once satisfied we were alone, he grabbed my shoulder and spun me around to shove me up against the door.

Before I could respond, he smashed his mouth against mine, a hand against the door on either side of my head, creating a cage around me. He nipped and licked at my lips but I refused to open to him, my body rigid and unresponsive. At least the majority of me stayed that way—below the waistband responded to his nearness, the spice of his cologne, and his demanding kiss. I tried getting my hands up to his chest to push him away, but there was no space between us, and he refused to budge.

Giving up on my mouth, Lance growled and kissed his way along my jaw to my ear. "C'mon, Danny, I'm real sorry about the other day and I've missed you. Just one kiss."

I moved my hand from his stomach to his crotch, and he wasn't kidding that he'd missed me. He was hard as a rock. He groaned when I squeezed the hard bulge. "You missed me, did you?"

He nodded against my neck and then pulled back to meet my eyes. "Yeah, I did. I haven't stopped thinking about you since I last saw you."

When he pressed his lips to mine again, I opened my mouth and invited his tongue in. While I let him set the pace of the kiss, I rubbed my thumb back and forth against his straining erection. I was excited to see him, and the fact that he was so eager to see me and kiss me only added to the enthusiasm. However, I'd had nothing but time to think of him over the previous four days and I needed to know. I wasn't about to let him get me all worked up and just leave me hanging again.

I kept my hand on his crotch; with the other, I reached up and wrapped my fingers around one of his wrists, pulled his hand down, and pressed it against my own hard prick.

I got my answer.

Lance jerked away and stumbled backwards, nearly tripping over his own feet. His eyes were wide, a panicked look on his face as he wiped a hand over his mouth.

"I thought so," I hissed. I reached behind me and turned the knob, opening the door without taking my eyes from him. "Get out."

He stood there clenching and unclenching the hand that had been pressed against my dick. That, combined with the expression on his face, flat-out infuriated me. "I said get the fuck out!" I roared.

My anger seemed to break through his shock and he took a step toward me. I sidestepped him and pulled the door open further, using it like a shield between us.

"I'm sorry. I just need a minute, is all."

"You don't need a minute. I can educate you in seconds flat. I'm a man. Not only am I a man, but a gay man. Not a chick, not some delicate girl you can seduce. A fucking man!" I pointed to the hallway. "Class dismissed."

His eyes darted to the hallway and he took a step. I thought he was going to leave, but just as I was ready to hit him in the ass with it, he grabbed the door with both hands, ripping it from my grip and slamming it shut. He then leaned back against it, blocking any escape I might have entertained.

"Danny, dammit, I'm sorry." He ran a hand through his hair. "I know you're a guy, I just…." The hand in his hair went around to the back of his neck, rubbing. "I just wasn't expecting that. That's all."

I crossed my arms over my chest and glared at him. "Expecting what? That a guy has a dick? You sure didn't have a problem with this *guy* touching yours."

Lance dropped his arm and his shoulders slumped. "Can we please just sit down and talk about this?" His eyes were pleading when he repeated, "Please?"

God, I was such a pushover. I stomped over to my bed and sat on the edge. I was tense, vibrating, and aching for a fight, but I'd let him at least say what he needed to before he left or I removed him.

He took a seat on Bo's bed, forearms resting on his knees, hands dangling as he stared at the floor between his feet. "I know what you are, Danny. I'm just having a really hard time dealing with it, is all.

When I'm not around you, I'm thinking about you all the fucking time: being with you, kissing you"—he raised his head and met my eyes— "touching you."

"The real thing not as good as the fantasies I take it?"

"No. I mean, yes... I mean...." He huffed out a breath. "Kissing you is way fucking better than any fantasy. It's just... I see you and you're like this gorgeous fucking chick and I get all hot and bothered and I know on some level you're a dude, but you don't look like a dude, but I know you are. And... and it's like that's a big part of what gets me so hot but, then I think, if I was attracted to guys then why the hell am I attracted to one that looks like...." He held his hand out, palm up.

He was rambling and I could tell how much his attraction to me was bothering him, but I kept my mouth shut. This was his shit to sort through. I probably could have been a little more sensitive, but dammit, it's a real ball-buster when you're kissing a guy and the minute he touches your dick, he runs. My ego was wounded.

He dropped his arm back to his knee and looked at me as if he were waiting for me to explain it all. After a few more minutes, he gave up and finally said, "I don't know what it was about that stripper. When I left the club, I couldn't think of anything but him and how I'd been turned on like I'd never been before. After I bailed on the guy I met on the Internet, I swore I'd never act on it again. Put it behind me like it was just part of growing up. That it didn't mean anything.

"But obviously it didn't stay in the past, because when I'm with you, it's the same kind of feeling. You drive me out of my head crazy, thinking about you. But I'm not going to lie, Danny. Just like with that stripper, my attraction to you freaks me the fuck out. I'm not gay." He shook his head vigorously, then stopped and hung his head. He sounded so miserable when he whispered, "Am I?"

My abused ego was petted and I relaxed a little. "So you found something that tripped your trigger in a big way. Maybe it's the thrill, the taboo of it, I don't really know. I learned a long time ago that we can't choose what or who we're attracted to, and there isn't always any rhyme or reason to it. If I had to take a guess, I'd say you're curious and there is nothing wrong with that."

He looked up at me and started to say something, but I hushed him by holding up a hand. "Although I may understand it's confusing the hell out of you, I gotta tell you. I'm not thrilled by your reaction to me."

"I'm sorry."

"Don't apologize for something you can't change. But you need to look at this from my point of view. While I may be incredibly flattered by your attraction to me—" I dramatically moved my hand down from head to toe, pointing out the goods. "I mean, what's not to be attracted to?"

That made him chuckle and some of the tension in the room dissipated. "True."

"That still doesn't change the fact of what I am. So you have to ask yourself, what are you going to do about your attraction? I'm game for a little exploration and fun, but I can tell you right now, I can't handle you getting all revved up and wanting to kiss me whenever you see me, getting me all worked up and then leaving me hanging. That's just cruel."

"I'm not sure what I can handle," he admitted quietly.

I leaned back on my elbows and stretched my legs out, crossing my ankles. "Then let's keep our interaction to waving hello in passing or chatting civilly when we're with Bo and Katie, until you figure it out."

"I know I don't want that."

I tipped my head back and blew out a breath. Good God, the man was going to drive me to drink. One more deep breath. "So what do you want from me, Lance? My turn for a little truth here. What I'd like to do with your sexy ass goes way beyond what's proper in public, but I'm not going to pretend I'm a chick to make you feel more comfortable with this. You can't have it both ways."

Lance stayed in the same position, head hanging, staring at the floor for long moments. It was a lot to think about, I knew that. I liked Lance well enough. He was a little strange at times, but he was hot and intriguing. I was a horny bastard and loved a challenge, so fuck yeah, I was more than willing to educate Lance on the awesomeness of male-on-male action. Friends with benefits worked well for me. However, I wasn't going to suck his dick or fuck him while he hid behind closed-eyed fantasies of being with a chick. If that's what he was looking for, he'd be better off looking for some little co-ed who was willing to strap one on.

Finally, after what seemed like hours—but was in actuality only minutes—Lance lifted his head, a smile curling his lips. "You think my ass is sexy?"

A small giggle escaped me since I wasn't expecting that response. I rolled my eyes as he waggled his brows at me. "It's not bad," I deadpanned.

He got up from where he was sitting on Bo's bed and moved to mine, sitting next to me. "You can't take it back now. You said, and I quote, 'your sexy ass'."

"Yeah, yeah, so we both seem to be attracted to each other. Question is, what are you going to do about it?"

Lance didn't answer with words. While he'd been quietly staring at the floor, he must have come to some conclusion, because he leaned in and pressed his mouth against mine. It started as a gentle brush of lips, no tongue or teeth—tender. I wasn't passive but I didn't set the pace either. Lance kissed my top lip, the corners of my mouth, and then pulled at my bottom lip with his. I hummed when he added his tongue into the mix. The sound must have encouraged him, as he thrust his tongue into my mouth and grabbed the back of my head, tangling his fingers in my hair, not letting me pull back from the kiss. He needn't have worried. I sucked at his tongue, adding mine into the battle, which pulled a moan from him as the kiss became more and more aggressive.

I wasn't gentle when I grabbed the back of his head in return and tugged at the silky strands, pulling him back and following him with my mouth. I pressed and pulled against his body until he was lying on his back and I was leaning down over him. My dick twitched in my jeans as my arousal renewed. I released the hold I had on his hair and ran my fingers along the thick tendon on the side of his neck, down his chest, and over the ridges of muscle on his stomach. I didn't stop until I reached the waistband of his jeans. I lifted his sweatshirt, the tips of my fingers seeking out the warm flesh beneath. He shuddered beneath me when I moved back up his body, my palm soft against his heated flesh. I reached up and pinched and tugged at his left nipple until it was an erect nub, and then moved to the right, giving it the same treatment, all the while kissing him.

When I ran my hand back down his chest, I pulled back to look at him. Lance's eyes were squeezed shut, his breathing labored through parted lips. I wanted to see his face, look into his eyes as I touched him and I wanted him to see *me*. "Open your eyes, Lance."

He slowly complied, blinking, his eyes heavy with lust.

"Keep them open," I murmured as I popped the button on his jeans.

He nodded; his breath hitched when I eased down his zipper and released his straining prick. "Ah, yeah," he moaned as his hips lifted off the bed when I wrapped my hand around his length and began stroking him.

"Feel good?"

"Fuck, yeah." He snapped his hips, pushing his dick through my fist. "Harder."

I set a rapid pace, stroking him from the flared, leaking cockhead, down to the base, and back up. He was leaking a steady stream of precum, slicking the way for my palm. A tremor went through him when I slowed my movements to press my thumb against his slit and then teased the wet digit around the underside of his engorged head. I set a rhythm of stroking and teasing until his cock began to throb in my hand, and I knew he was close. I stroked downward to the base and squeezed. Lance's eyes darkened further, the black of his pupils nearly blowing out all traces of color, and he breathed harshly, trying to control his need to come.

With Lance's focus on his pleasure, I knew it was the perfect opportunity to see how far he was willing to go with his new resolve. I shifted until I could reach the button of my jeans. Unfastening my pants, I shoved the denim down my hips, releasing my own painfully hard cock. Lance's brow creased, but he didn't say anything and he didn't push me away. He kept his eyes locked with mine as I laid back down next to him, propping myself up on an elbow, facing him. Encouraged, I pumped him a couple of times, moving him closer to the edge of his orgasm, keeping his focus on his pleasure, before saying, "Touch me, Lance." I kissed him hard, demanding his full attention until he moaned and thrust hard. "Only a touch," I whispered against his parted lips, my hand still working him hard.

One of Lance's large hands wrapped around mine, squeezing, forcing my grip to tighten. I was just about to tell him that wasn't what I had meant, when his other hand shot out, grabbed my dick. He began pumping me in harmony with the fast rhythm we set on his own cock.

It didn't take long before Lance threw his head back, spine arching, and he grunted as liquid heat fountained up over our joined hands and landed on his stomach. Watching him chase his pleasure, his calloused hand causing the perfect friction along my length, and the smell of sex pulled my orgasm from my body.

I collapsed back onto the bed, pulse racing as I worked to catch my breath. Lance continued to stroke me; his hand had gentled but even that became too much on my overly sensitive prick and I pushed his hand away. To my utter disbelief, he rolled over until he was the one looking down at me, a big satisfied grin on his face.

"That was so fucking hot!" Then he kissed me and laughed. "Let's do that again."

So much for him having an issue with touching a guy. I grabbed his wrist before he could take me back in hand. "Jesus. Give me a minute," I groaned, still breathing hard.

His smile turned mischievous and he winked. "Okay, I'll give you five."

I closed my eyes before I could roll them. What the hell had I just created?

CHAPTER
seven

IN MICHIGAN there have always been three seasons: football, baseball, and winter. Winters suck; rarely did enough snow accumulate to really do many of the fun things like sledding, skiing, or snowmobiling. Usually in southern Michigan, it was just cold and miserable. You had to go to the Upper Peninsula or Canada to really get the full snow effect. Back in the eighties, there was a hell of a snowstorm. The freeways shut down and people were stuck in their homes for a couple of weeks. The road crews just couldn't keep up with the amount of white stuff being dumped on the state. I was conceived during that crazy storm. However, since my childhood, I don't remember—much to my regret while a kid—ever having snow like that.

With the temperatures hovering around the twenty-degree mark but no snow, most activities are done inside. Classes were in full swing during February so it's not like I could head to a state with warmer climate, even if I could afford it. Lance and I, however, were not bored. He wasn't playing ball, and we'd set up a routine since the new semester had started. Anytime Bo was with Katie, Lance was with me. We hadn't gone past kissing and mutual jerk off, but he was beginning to get a lot more comfortable with me, behind closed doors anyway. It no longer bothered him on the nights when he showed up that I had a clean face and old sweats and T-shirt. I think we were actually starting to like each other beyond the physical attraction.

One night Lance showed up unannounced. I was lying on my bed reading a script from *West Side Story*. I had an audition later in the week and I really, really wanted the lead role of the young protagonist, Tony. It didn't surprise me when there was a hard knock on the door and it was Lance. We hadn't had the chance to see each other in nearly two weeks and if he was feeling anything like I was, he was beyond ready.

"Hey, c'mon in." I moved out of the way and ushered him in. "I wasn't expecting to see you tonight."

"Neither was I."

Lance pulled me to him and wrapped his arms around me before pressing our lips together. The kiss started out soft, but he wasted no time in deepening it, and I was only too happy to allow him.

"Fuck, I missed you," he said against my lips. "Been going out of my goddamn head," he continued as he kissed his way across my jaw.

I got all kinds of tingly when he admitted how much he'd missed me. I told myself it was just my horny hormones causing the sensation and that it absolutely did not have anything to do with how he held me or the way his tender kisses tasted just slightly sweeter than the harder ones.

Since I hadn't been expecting to see him, nor had I planned to leave the dorm, I hadn't shaved that day. I tensed slightly in anticipation of him pulling away when his lips came in contact with the stubble, but to my surprise, he didn't. Not only did he not pull away, he seemed to spend an extra amount of time kissing and teasing my jaw. Yeah, he was definitely getting used to the fact I was a guy. I guess I should have figured that one out a while back by the way he seemed so fascinated by my dick.

He spent an inordinate amount of time touching it, pulling, stroking, studying it, and I had to believe he could describe every bump, ridge, and vein from memory. Long after we got off and had cleaned up the mess, he trailed his fingers gently over my length, like most lovers trailed their fingers over a hip or the sinew of a back. He still hadn't gone beyond touch, no lips to dick, either given or received, but I wasn't complaining. I had never been with anyone who loved to snuggle as much as Lance. His touch could ignite me one moment and soothe me the next. I was becoming addicted to his touch, was content for the time being, and didn't push for more. I knew that eventually he'd move us to the next step when he was ready.

Lance made it down to my shoulder, pulled the material of my T-shirt to the side, and grunted. "Even my mark is fading."

My head rolled to the side when he began sucking up a mark, worrying the skin with both lips and teeth until it began to ache. Still he continued to suck hard, like he was trying to permanently leave his mark. "That's enough. I'm pretty sure I'm marked properly."

His arms tightened around me and he seemed to suck even harder.

When it became too much, I pushed him away. "Damn, you're like a leech,"

He met my eyes, the gray orbs looking a little glazed for a minute until he got himself under control. "Sorry, guess I got a little carried away."

"No shit."

"Sorry. Just making sure my mark stays where it belongs." As his eyes landed on the mark on my neck that was now throbbing, he didn't look the least bit sorry. And truth be told, I wasn't sorry either. I liked having his mark on me, but just like the tender kisses, I chalked it up to being randy.

The smile on his face was way too smug as he studied his work, like maybe he liked it there as much as I did and maybe, just maybe, he was doing it to claim me. I pushed those insane thoughts away when he added, "Plus—" He licked his lips. "—you taste so damn good."

"You're getting a little weird on me, dude. You got some kind of vampire fetish I should know about?"

I moved past him, planning to plop back down on my bed, but he grabbed my wrist, stopping my movement. He pulled me against him, this time with my back against his chest, and his arms around me, pinning my arms against my body. He gently pressed his mouth to the mark and asked, "You want me to?"

"Uh, let me think about it. No!" I squirmed out of his arms. "No biting."

"But nibbling is still okay, right?"

"Nibbling is most definitely still okay and encouraged." I got a huge grin for that. I grabbed the script I'd been reading and set it on Bo's desk before crawling up on the bed and leaning back against the headboard. "I take it Bo's with Katie?"

"Don't know," he said as he joined me on the bed. He stretched out next to me, his back facing the wall, and laid his head in my lap. "I tried calling both Katie and Bo but neither of them are answering their phones. I think the storm might have knocked out the tower or is interrupting the reception." He traced his fingers along the outside of my thigh and I shivered.

Then it hit me what he said. "Storm? What storm?" I hadn't been listening to the radio all day, instead playing the soundtrack to *West Side Story* to get in the mood while I read, and I hadn't been outside since the day before. The last I'd heard, we were expecting a couple of inches but the bulk of the storm would be hitting way north of us.

"Yeah, they're calling it the storm of the decade. Expecting ten to twelve inches tonight and even more tomorrow."

"What the hell? I hadn't heard anything about the storm hitting here?"

He lifted his head and met my eyes. "You know, you should come out of your fantasy world once in a while. They've been predicting it's going to hit us for the last two days."

His hand moved from the outside of my thigh, across my hip, until he ran a single finger down the length of my hardening shaft. It twitched in response to his touch. I arched a brow at him. "Look who's talking."

"Fantasy?" He cupped my entire dick in his palm and squeezed. "This feels pretty real to me."

"Nope, just a figment of your imagination."

He pushed up my shirt and pressed a kiss just below my navel, my pulse speeding in response to his warm, soft lips and breath. He traced a path up my stomach with the tip of his tongue, swirling it around and teasing my navel before moving up to my breastbone. "You taste real," he murmured against my flesh.

My entire body was tingling in response to his attention, my voice a little breathy when I said, "Nope, you're stuck in one of your daydreams."

Lance pushed my shirt all the way up, exposing my chest, the cool air of the room and his warm breath collided and goose bumps bloomed along my skin. I bit down on my lip to keep from crying out when he nipped and teased first one nipple, and then the other. He was practically lying on top of me, his hand steadily caressing my cock, by the time he reached my mouth.

All thoughts of teasing fled as he took my mouth in an all-consuming kiss. The heat and possessiveness made my blood boil and I needed more. I reached down and undid his jeans, doing my best to get his cock free and push the denim down his hips, but from the position I was in, it was nearly impossible and I groaned my frustration.

Lance pulled back slightly, kissed my pouting lips, and then sat back on his heels. "Need some help there?"

I made an incoherent noise in my throat that really meant "fuck off" or "yes please" and shoved down my sweats. My eyes were glued to his more-than-ample prick. The sight of it, hard and straining out from his body, made my mouth water. God, his dick was gorgeous. Not exceptionally long, but thick, the veins running along its length prominent, infused with blood. He was cut, and the slit glistened with precum.

Lance grabbed his cock and stroked sensually down its entire length; the visual delight and the sound of his deep, rumbling chuckle stirred me into action. I was so fucking horny. I sat up and, in one deft movement, had him on his back. I covered his body with my own and hissed when our cocks came in contact.

Whatever Lance was about to say died in his throat when I pressed my groin harder against his and began grinding our shafts together. I swear to God his eyes rolled back in his head as our wet cockheads slid back and forth, creating a delicious friction. I arched my back, hands gripping his shoulders, and watched the bliss on his face as I set a slow, sensual rhythm.

It wasn't long before the heat of our bodies had perspiration dampening my brow. A single drop rolled down my temple and landed on his heaving chest. I leaned down and licked the small drop from his chest, then worked my mouth up to his neck, kissing and licking the salt from his skin as my hands moved from his shoulders to his biceps, kneading and massaging the bulging muscles of his arms. I stretched out until we were pressed from toe to chest, keeping the same slow rhythm of my thrusts. Once his hands were above his head, I entwined our fingers and pressed my lips to his.

Lance immediately opened and I took control of the kiss as well, licking his lips, his teeth, sucking on his tongue.

Lance's hips began to snap and I pulled back just enough to whisper against his lips, "Be still, just let me make you feel good."

"Ah, Jesus, Danny. Never felt—" He gritted his teeth, breathing heavily through his nose, and I could tell he was trying to hold back his orgasm.

I rolled my hips then thrust hard. "Like that?"

"Fuck!" he growled, the sound deep and harsh. "You keep that up and I'm going to come." His back bowed and he panted, "Ah! What are you doing to me?"

God! I knew. I could hear it, the grunts and hoarse groans. I could see it in his eyes. He was seeing *me*. Not the dolled-up feminine façade he'd first been attracted to, but me, without makeup, and stubble on my chin. He saw me, Daniel Anderson Marshal, man. The look in his eyes told me he liked what he saw, and my fucking chest squeezed so tight I could barely breathe. His body felt so good against mine and he was so gorgeous in his pleasure that I could have come just from watching him. I didn't want this moment to end, but I couldn't not move and I couldn't look away. I was whimpering and writhing against him.

I was so hard, so fucking hard, I knew I wasn't going to last much longer, but that was okay because I knew he was close too. My balls drew up, and every muscle in my body coiled tightly, readying for release. "Come for me, Lance. Show me what I'm doing to you."

Lance gripped my hands tightly to the point of pain and cried out, wet heat spreading out between our bodies. I let go of the reins I'd been keeping on my orgasm, and with two more hard thrusts I was coming, riding hard against his cock until every drop was pulled from me. I collapsed onto him and buried my face in his neck.

Lance pulled his hands free from mine and wrapped both arms around me, holding me tightly as we both fought to catch our breaths. I felt more content and satisfied than I had in a very long time. The kissing and mutual jerk-off with him was fun and hot but I hadn't realized how much I missed the way a muscular body felt beneath me, against me, as I chased my orgasm. The friction, the heat, the slide of sweat-damp bodies working in sync to achieve release. I also came to another realization. It wasn't just the physical act that had me so content and satisfied; it was Lance. But I forced myself not to think too deeply about it, because quite honestly, that new bit of information scared the hell out of me. So I pushed it away and focused on my breathing and the sound of Lance's and how good I felt lying against him.

I knew I should get up and at least clean up the mess on our stomachs and chests, but I was enjoying the afterglow too much, and Lance didn't seem to be in any hurry to release me. One of his hands had moved up and was stroking my hair, the other drawing random patterns on my back. I closed my eyes and melted further into him.

When I woke an hour later, we were on our sides facing each other. One of us had pulled the afghan from the end of the bed over us, but we were still pressed close to each other, my head resting on Lance's bicep. My bladder was screaming at me to get up, but I didn't want to move. It felt so amazing being in his arms and I was worried this would be a one-time thing. A jolt went through me when I realized I hoped it wouldn't be. Lying there looking at him, so peaceful, and feeling so warm and content, it was hard to think of him as nothing more than a fuck buddy, but I had to.

Lance and I had nothing in common beyond the walls of this room. He lived and breathed football. Except for the pants the players wore, I loathed the sport. I was happiest when visiting the theater or art museum. Better yet, performing on a stage. And as for Lance, he…. Well, he liked football. Eventually, whatever it was Lance and I had together, it would end. I looked forward to the times we spent together, but I knew I'd want more. For now, it worked for both of us, our busy lives not allowing for any more. I needed to convince myself that this was all there ever would be for the two of us, and if I was smart, I'd keep my heart firmly locked away.

Careful not to wake him, I extricated myself from his limbs and got to my feet. The mystery of the afghan was solved as I looked down at his sleeping form. Somehow, I'd managed to pull up my sweats and cover us. Lance's jeans were still around his thighs, sweatshirt pushed up and the dried remnants of our orgasms obvious on his belly. As I continued to stare at him, my cock began to fill. He looked so good sprawled out there before me like a feast.

I wasn't sure when Bo would return. We'd been lucky we weren't caught and I wasn't about to push our luck. I covered him, grabbed my cell phone from the desk and some clean clothes from the dresser. I smelled like sex and Lance. While I loved the scent, I wasn't sure I wanted to explain my new aroma to my roommate. Before quietly stepping out, I grabbed my shower bag and towel and closed the door behind me.

Once in the hall, I checked my cell, but there were no new messages. I only made it a few steps down the hall when the door to Mike's room opened and he stepped out. "Hey, Danny, hell of a storm, eh?"

"Yeah. You wouldn't happen to have cell service, would you?"

"Nope. Internet is down too."

"Damn! I haven't heard from Bo all day. Have you seen him?"

Mike leaned back against his door and shifted the large brown bag he had to his other arm. "Nope. I haven't seen him all week. Lucky bastard is probably holed up somewhere with his new squeeze."

"Probably." I hoped so anyway. "I'll see you later."

I started to walk away when Mike pushed off from the door and walked with me. "A bunch of us are meeting down in the student lounge. Going to make some hot toddies, want to join us?" He leaned in a little and murmured, "Best to be in a group if the power goes out. We can share body heat."

I had to fight not to wrinkle my nose in disgust and keep my face neutral. Mike had moved into the dorm the same time I had and he'd been propositioning me ever since. Nice guy, but yeah, I'm shallow enough to admit that the pus-filled zits that covered his face were a major turn off. The thought of him kissing me, getting close to those festering things, just tripped my gag reflex.

"I'm going to get a quick shower in case the power does go out and I'll think about it." Before he could respond, I quickened my steps to get away from him, calling out over my shoulder, "Talk to you later."

Not a fucking chance. I had all the body heat I needed waiting for me back in my bed.

chapter
eight

THE small lamp on Bo's desk cast a subdued light on Lance's still-sleeping form when I stepped back into my dorm room. He was in the same position I'd left him, the scent of sweat and sex powerful in the room. Bo was sure to know what the hell had been going on the minute he walked in, and that was a conversation I wasn't ready to have. Bo wasn't stupid. He knew there was something going on between Lance and me, but I didn't want to give any proof to his suspicions.

I threw my dirty clothes in the closet, returned the shower bag to its place on the shelf, sat down at my vanity, and lit the hazelnut candle. If the nutty aroma was enough to cover up the stink of Bo's feet, it would be more than sufficient to eradicate the smell of man sex. I wasn't sure why I didn't want Bo to know about Lance and me. We never kept shit from each other, but for some reason, I just wasn't ready to share this with him yet. Perhaps it was the fact he was dating Lance's sister, or because I knew Lance wouldn't want him to know and it wasn't my place to out him. Whatever the reason, I was willing to keep it to myself for now.

I scrubbed the towel over my head, then dropped it on the floor and grabbed a brush. As I ran it through my hair, I contemplated putting on makeup. I didn't normally go through the trouble just to sit around my room, but I could tell Lance really liked when I wore it. The fact I was even contemplating putting it on made me scowl at my reflection in the mirror. What the hell was wrong with me? Why should I care what Lance thought? We'd already gotten off, so he'd be leaving as soon as he woke. He never stayed too long after an orgasm.

A rustling sound caught my attention and I turned my head to find Lance staring at me as he pulled up his jeans. "What time is it?"

"Seven."

He yawned and then stretched before sitting back against the headboard. "Your bed sucks."

"Oh, really?" I arched a brow at him. "You didn't seem to have any problem snoring in it."

He laughed. "I just meant it's too small." He held out his arms. "C'mere."

I hesitated. I think I was in shock; it's the only reason I can think of that had me up out of my chair and moving to the bed without so much as a single word. Once I was close enough, Lance grabbed my hand, pulled me down on top of him, and pressed a soft, tender kiss to my lips. Still stunned, I clung to him as he kissed my chin, along my jaw, and down my neck, leaving me a little breathless and tingly when he stopped.

"You always wake up in a good mood?"

"Not normally, but never as cranky as you do."

I swatted at him playfully, making him laugh. Another thing I was getting addicted to. I loved his laugh. He shifted me until I was lying on my side between him and the wall, my head resting on his chest. With his free hand, he grabbed the remote from the desk and switched on the TV, but there was nothing but static and white noise.

"Internet and cable are down. Storm's getting worse. We'll be lucky if we don't lose power."

"Damn. I was hoping to ride out the storm with a good show. You have anything besides *Star Trek*?"

"I think Bo has a collection of *Star Wars* too."

Lance hit the Mute button and groaned. "That's almost as bad."

"Well, I do have…." I bit my lip to stop the rest of the words from passing my lips.

"You have what?"

"Nothing." It wasn't the fact that I had porn that had me hesitating, it was the sheer amount—along with some of the naughtier titles—that had me hiding my heated cheeks in his chest.

Lance rolled slightly and cupped my chin, forcing me to look at him. "I'm guessing from your reaction and the color in your cheeks we're not talking about a collection of musicals?"

I pursed my lips and refused to say anything.

"Danny, do you have a collection of porn you're trying to hide from me?"

Shit! I never did have a filter between my brain and mouth and I regretted that flaw even more with the knowing look Lance gave me. "Fine," I said with a huff. "I have a couple of DVDs but nothing you'd be interested in."

His brows rose and his grin turned to a smirk.

"Whatever." I pushed his hand away from my face. "Even if you were interested in them, I'm not about to put one in. We don't know if Bo is going to show up or not. Speaking of Bo, don't you think you should move to his bed, just in case he does come home?"

"No way in hell he's coming home in this shit. I barely made it in myself and that was over two hours ago. So about those videos?"

"Just don't say I didn't warn you."

I crawled over him and went to the closet. I pulled the box down that I stored them in and started rummaging through it. There were a shit load of burned amateur DVDs that Lee had shared with me—*Bondage Boy* and *Homemade Rough Stuff*—that I sure as hell wasn't about to pull out, and shoved them beneath the purchased ones. It wasn't anything I wanted to try, even if I had gotten horny as hell when I'd watched them, it didn't mean I wanted that stuff done to me. I certainly didn't want to give Lance the wrong impression. Which titles like, *Twins*, *Down on the Farm*, and *Gang Bang Slam* were sure to do. I grabbed the first purchased one, *Pool Party*, and quickly added that one to the burned ones. Lance was so not ready for double-penetration videos.

"What's taking you so long? Damn, how big is your collection?"

"Shut up," I called back. I pulled out one called *The Bachelor's Party*. It wasn't too bad. A hot tub blowjob scene, a three-way, but nothing too kinky. I put the box back on the self, my heart rate increasing when I stepped out with the movie.

I started to walk past the TV, intending to give it to Lance to check out, but he obviously wanted to do more than read the cover when he said, "Put it in."

Damn!

"What's up with your sudden interest in my porn collection?" I popped open the case and pulled out the DVD and shook it at him.

"Oh, so it's an entire collection now, is it?"

I thought about throwing the damn thing at his smug face, but it was one of my favorites so I settled for rolling my eyes at him and inserted it into the player.

I joined Lance back on the bed, sitting with my back against the wall, legs tucked up under me, just as he hit Play.

"You don't want to cuddle me while we watch?"

"I've seen it. I think I'll enjoy watching your reaction more than the flick."

"That bad?"

"Not if you like hot ass-licking and fucking."

Lance wrinkled his nose and I laughed. He had mentioned he'd gone to a gay club but hadn't gone in. He'd also talked to a guy on the Internet and thought about meeting him, but again had backed out at the last minute. Was it even possible that he'd never even seen a gay porn video? I was betting that he would back out on the film as well.

The video started out innocently enough, just a couple of guys sitting at a table, but the TV was still muted so you couldn't hear what they were saying. "You know, this is a lot better with the volume turned up."

He didn't respond, eyes glued to the TV, but he unmuted it.

After a brief scene where the actors talked about a party they had recently attended, the setting changed to one of the men's memories. Two men were lying on a white coverlet atop a king-size bed, shirtless and kissing.

I pulled up my legs, wrapped my arms around them, and laid my head on my knees. My full attention was focused on Lance's face as he watched the show.

At first, he didn't seem to react at all, but I could tell when things started to get a little more physical on the screen by the way Lance began to behave. His breathing sped up slightly and he set the remote aside. He swallowed hard and one of his hands went to his chest. Lance had pulled his jeans up but hadn't fastened them, and I could see the head of his cock beginning to push at his boxers. I stole a quick glance at the screen. One of the men licked and teased the other man's nipple, pulling it between his bright white teeth until the guy arched his back and cried out. They were both now completely naked. Was that what had Lance's breath speeding up? Had it turned him on watching these two burly men undress? Or perhaps it had been the kissing. Lance loved to kiss, and lucky for me, he was damn good at it.

I turned my attention back to Lance. He was rubbing his hand back and forth across his chest and pinching his nipples through the cotton of his sweatshirt. The way he never even blinked, eyes glued to the TV, I had no doubt Lance's hand was following the same path as the actor's.

Lance moved downward, rubbing and caressing his stomach as the moaning on the screen increased, the tip of his pinkie just barely brushing against the head of his cock. Blood rushed to my groin and my dick twitched against my hip. I sucked in my bottom lip and held it between my teeth, holding back my own moan, but it was no use when his waistband was pushed down, exposing his engorged and wet-with-precum cockhead. A small sound escaped me and it was enough to pull Lance's attention from the screen. His heated gaze met mine and he instantly snatched his underwear back up, cheeks going red.

"I…. Um…."

Lance was getting off on it, and I wasn't about to let a little embarrassment ruin the mood. I reached out and stroked his hard length through the cotton material and covered his mouth with mine. Lance was so hard against my palm; I could feel his rapid pulse racing through the thick veins. His discomfort at being caught enjoying the movie forgotten, he grabbed the back of my head, hand tightening in my hair, tugging, sending sparks of pain across my scalp as he controlled the kiss. Christ, he was ruthless, fucking my mouth with his tongue. I had no doubt he could have come just from the pressure of my hand on his dick and the assault on my mouth, but I wanted more than a mutual masturbation session. I wanted to taste him.

I had seen *The Bachelor's Party* enough times, I knew exactly what was happening on the screen by the wet sucking noises emitting from the TV. I pried his fingers from my hair and kissed my way down his chin and then to his Adam's apple. The deep rumbling sound he made as I nipped and sucked at his throat vibrated against my tongue.

I didn't linger but moved steadily down his body, licking a path from his navel to his groin and pulling another harsh sound from him that I felt in my dick. Lance wasn't the only one who was close. Just watching him react to the film, the way he'd absently touched himself, had me aching.

Lance took in a harsh breath when I placed a kiss on the head of his prick, the sound growing louder when I licked at his slit. Fuck, he tasted amazing, bitter and musky, and I wanted more. I sucked the flared head into my mouth, tongue swirling as I pushed his jeans down his hips for better access to his entire length.

"Ah, Christ, that feels good," Lance moaned.

I lifted my eyes to find him staring at me, his kiss-swollen lips parted. I pulled back just enough that his wet cock was against my lips when I spoke. "You're missing the movie." I licked him again, blowing my warm breath against the sensitive head, causing him to shudder.

His eyes flicked to the screen, then settled back on me. He pressed his palm against my cheek; his thumb teased the side of my mouth, his gentle touch at such odds with how wound up he seemed to be. "It can't hold my attention when I have you to watch."

I lowered my head slowly until I took him into my throat—thank God for no gag reflex—and swallowed.

"Holy fuck!" Lance groaned, the strangled sound echoing off the walls of the small room. I glanced up to see his eyes wide in disbelief.

I loved to give head and was damn good at it. From Lance's reaction, I knew he'd never had anyone give him a proper blowjob and no way would he last long. I shoved down my sweats and stroked myself. I bobbed my head, taking him deep, then back up till just the head was past my lips, then slowly down the entire length. He was close, his body vibrating, breaths harsh. I increased the speed of my hand, pumping hard and fast as I planned to step over the edge into bliss with him.

As I continued to suck him, I reached over and cupped his balls, gently tugging and massaging. Lance gasped and grabbed the back of my skull in his palm. At first he only held it against my head, but then he went wild beneath me, squirming and thrusting, seizing my hair in his fist.

"Oh. Oh fuck." His back arched, his muscles tensing further. "Danny… better stop," he tried warning me, but I wasn't going to be denied. I sucked harder.

Give it to me. I pulled back when I felt him swell further against my tongue, until just the flared head was in my mouth and I hungrily feasted on his flesh. I squeezed at the base of my own dick, not wanting to come until Lance was sated. The first burst of hot cream on my tongue was my undoing. I greedily swallowed every drop, and the pressure I'd added to my shaft wasn't enough to hold back my orgasm as Lance's flavor filled my mouth. I breathed harshly through my nose and whimpered, unwilling to release his still-throbbing cock while I shot burst after burst over Lance leg.

I felt Lance's body go slack, and only then did I let his prick slip from my mouth. The death grip he had on my hair loosened and then fell away.

I licked the small drop of cum from the corner of my mouth and crawled up the bed to lie next to him. I reached over, snatched up the remote and turned off the TV, the room falling into darkness. I kissed his chest before laying my head upon it. "Damn, I can't wait to act out the next scene. You taste amazing."

I must have sucked out his ability to speak along with his orgasm, because he let out a nervous laugh and patted my hip. "I'll need a little recovery time here, Danny."

I could only imagine what his comment would have been if I'd told him the next scene included a double-headed dildo.

CHAPTER
nine

THE winter of my sophomore year in college, at the time, seemed like one of the best periods of my life. I'd spent three full days snowed in with Lance, getting to know him. I learned that he was so much more than a dumb jock as I'd originally thought. I'd accused him of not being the brightest crayon in the box, which was unfair. Lance worked his ass off with tutors to maintain the C average needed to be eligible to play football. Dyslexia made it all the more difficult for him. However, he'd been playing football since he was big enough to throw a ball, and he had a passion for it. His passion helped him seize a full-ride scholarship to the University of Michigan; otherwise he'd be playing for one of the smaller schools. His parents were hard-working, took good care of their children, but could never have afforded to send them to college. They must have instilled their hard-work standards in both of their children, because Katie had also gotten a scholarship, hers based on academics rather than athletics.

Lance's dream was that his passion and his strong work ethic would take him all the way to the NFL one day. Beyond that, he had no Plan B.

There was also so much more to him. Beneath the cocky jock-boy persona was a hell of a nice guy with a lot of charm who was witty as hell. He loved to cuddle when he slept, which was a huge plus for me. He was devoted to his family and friends. I also learned Lance and Katie weren't just close siblings—they were twins. It explained why he was so close to her and why he wanted to know and interact with those in her life. However, it didn't explain his fascination with me.

I wasn't complaining.

During our snowbound days, Lance went from being obsessed with touching my dick to having my lips touch his. He'd had plenty of blowjobs prior to our hooking up, but never one as good as I gave, and yeah, I admit, I liked being the best. When he didn't have his dick shoved down my throat or we weren't rubbing off, jerking off, or kissing, we were eating or playing cards. We completely wiped out Bo's stash of junk food his mom was always sending him that he kept stored under his bed, and played no less than a thousand games of double solitaire. It was either that or watch Bo's collection of DVDs, and that was a huge no-fucking-way for me.

I'm pretty sure it was during those three days that my heart threw out the memo that it was not to get attached to Lance. The way he would touch me was like nothing I'd ever experienced before. I'd woken one morning to find him gently stroking my hair, looking at me with this… I'm not sure how to describe the look. Awe, wonderment. All I do know was that it stole my fucking breath. It was after we were finally shoveled out that everything began to change.

The first few weeks were fine. Lance would come over every chance he got to satisfy his new favorite pastime, and I was satisfied to have a new fuck buddy. Well, I guess I couldn't really call him a fuck buddy, since we weren't fucking, but I had hope. I knew Lance was trying to come to terms with his attraction for me, so I was patient. My insane schedule didn't allow me to worry over how my feelings for Lance were changing. Running around like a chicken with its head cut off, trying to fit thirty-six hours into twenty-four, doesn't leave much time to think about such things.

Mid-March was busy—ramped up to beyond busy—yeah, no big surprise there. To my great delight and that of my parents, I'd snagged the lead role in *West Side Story*. My dad had also starred as Tony when he was in college, so it was important that I give my all to this new family tradition.

Wednesdays were a total bitch for me. I had three classes, voice coach, and then rehearsal. I'd just gotten back from the theater one Wednesday night and the minute I had my coat and shoes off, I dove onto my bed. I had plans to nap for an hour and then spend the rest of the night cramming for an exam I had the next morning on the conceptualization of a play, when my phone rang. I ignored both it and the beep indicating I had a message. The second sequence of rings and beep had me groaning and pulling my tired ass up from the bed to power the son of a bitch off.

Just as I pulled it from my coat pocket, it rang again.

"What," I snapped without looking at the display screen.

"Whoa, someone sounds a bit cranky."

"You have no idea."

"Would it help if I told you I missed you?" Lance asked.

I sat on the edge of the bed and ran a hand over my burning eyes. "Probably not. I'm too exhausted to care."

"Aw, c'mon, Danny. It's been five days since I've seen you, and if I know you, you haven't eaten. Let me take you out to dinner."

He was right. I hadn't had anything but half of a stale bagel earlier that morning and my stomach growled at the prospect of food. My body, however, said, "Not going to happen." I flopped back on the bed and rested my head on the pillow. "I'm too tired to go out. How about you bring dinner here?"

"Um…. Well…."

"Well what?" Exhaustion made my voice abrasive.

After a minute of silence, Lance finally said, "How about a drive-through? We can eat in the car and then I'll bring you back."

"What part of *tired* don't you understand? Why can't you just pick up something? Work with me here."

"I'm already halfway there."

This meant he'd just passed McDonald's two minutes ago. Heaven forbid he'd have to turn around. My aching feet and weary muscles argued with my grumbling gut, but finally my hunger won out over the need for sleep. I could have saved myself some grief and grabbed something from Bo's restocked junk food, but I did miss Lance. "All right. How long?"

"Five."

"I'll meet you out front."

I slipped on my tennis shoes and grabbed my coat. I didn't bother with hat and scarf; I was getting door-to-door service. Lance was sitting at the curb halfway to the end of the building. *So much for door-to-*

door. I wrapped my coat tighter around me and jogged to his car, nearly ass-planting when I hit a patch of ice. I caught myself and cursed the lack of traction on my Converse, then threw in a ripe curse for Lance for making me walk.

"What the hell?" I asked when I slid into his car. "You couldn't park any farther away?"

"Uh, yeah, sorry about that." He put the car in drive. "Someone was parked there when I first got here."

I thought his statement and the tone of his voice was a little odd. It had taken me less than five minutes to get from my room to the front and I hadn't seen anyone pulling away. I just shrugged, too out of it to question him about it. At least he'd been considerate enough to have the heat on full blast.

"So what do you feel like eating?"

"Anything is fine."

Lance nodded and pulled out onto the road. "You look good," he said, stealing a glance my way.

I hadn't bothered to shower or wash my face when I'd gotten home, so I was still in full, crazy summer look, with yellow, pink, purple, and green eye shadows and half-false lashes. Yeah, I know it was only March and summer was months away. But by that time of year in Michigan, you are so over winter.

"Thanks. You look good too."

And he did. Lance had been letting his hair grow out, his bangs now shaggy brown waves over his forehead, a short trimmed dark beard covered his jaw. So, so rugged, and sexy, he never failed to get my blood rushing.

After grabbing a couple of double cheeseburger meals, his super-sized of course, Lance drove to the parking garage instead of back to the dorm.

"What are we doing here?"

"Just thought we'd eat before it got cold is all."

I cocked my head at him, brows going up. He was acting so weird, but I didn't call him on it.

The garage was deserted that time of night but he parked at the back, away from any overhead lights. Once he put the car in park, I passed out the food, then leaned back against the door and munched on a fry.

"This is cozy. A little dark, but cozy."

I could barely make Lance out—the only light in the car was from the display on the radio—but I saw him shrug. "Yeah, just you and me," he said around a mouth full of food.

"I did tell you Bo wasn't home, right?"

"Mmm hmm." He washed down the bite he'd taken with his soda. "With how tired you've been, I worried about you dying. So I just saved your life."

"Dying?"

"Yeah. If I fed you in your bed, you'd probably pass out midbite and end up choking to death." Even in the low light I could see his wide, bright white smile. "You're welcome."

"Whatever." But I couldn't help but laugh.

"How's the play coming along?"

"Really good, but very tiring. I'm so ready for opening night. Are you coming?"

"Of course. I wouldn't miss seeing you as a street-smart punk." He hesitated for moment then asked, "You think they'll let you wear those spike knee-high boots? Those are so sexy."

"You know, Lance," I said dryly, "keep up the jokes and I'll ban you from the theater." I threw a fry at him.

He batted it away before it could hit him and laughed.

We finished our meal in silence, the only sounds a classic rock tune playing low on the radio and Lance slurping his drink and smacking his food. I shook my head. The man really needed that class on dinner etiquette.

"I bet you're really sleepy now that your belly is full, huh?" he asked and handed me his garbage to add to the bag at my feet. "Can I at least get a kiss before I take you back?"

"I don't know. I'm pretty tired," I teased.

Lance grabbed my wrist and pulled me across the car, his other hand going behind my head to tangle in my hair. He brushed his lips over mine and whispered against them, "Let me see if I can wake you up."

I licked at his lips, encouraging him to deepen the kiss, an invitation he took without hesitation, and plunged his tongue in. I laid my hand on his thigh, my fingertips teasing the inside seam of his jeans. He moaned, dropped my wrist, and placed his hand over mine, encouraging me to move up higher until I was cupping his hard bulge. As he explored my mouth, I ran my hand over his denim-covered dick, pressing against it with my palm.

"Fuck yeah," he muttered when I popped the button on his pants. "Touch me, Danny." He kissed me again. "Missed you touching me."

I carefully eased down his zipper and shoved my hand inside, gripping his cock tightly, and stroked from base to crown and back down. He must have been thinking about this while we ate, since he was rock hard, throbbing, and already seeping from the tip, slicking the way. I kissed my way across his jaw, the coarse hairs tickling my lips. I spent some time licking and nipping at his chin before moving down his throat.

"You really have missed me, haven't you?" I asked before biting down on his shoulder, and then sucking the abused area hard. I don't remember when this ritual began or why, but Lance and I always marked each other when we were together. I'm sure if I had thought too hard about it, it would have scared me, but I never did.

Lance jerked, and then pushed up into my hand, fucking my fist hard and fast. "Yeah, I did," he panted.

"Mmm. I can tell."

The hand on the back of my head moved to my shoulder and I felt him press down. "Suck me, Danny."

I allowed him to steer me toward his dick, and I placed a kiss to the glistening crown, lapping at the precum. As his flavor filled my mouth, my dick twitched as it swelled to full hardness. I licked my way down his shaft, followed the thick veins, and slowly back up, teasing his slit before sucking the wide head into my mouth.

"Ah, God, Danny. Love your mouth on me."

I felt Lance grow impossibly larger in my mouth, could feel his leg shaking beneath my hand. I sucked harder, the tip of my tongue teasing the little ridge just below the head. He was moaning, incoherent words flowing from his mouth.

Then, without warning, Lance grabbed the back of my head and shoved at the same time he thrust upward. He caught me off guard and I nearly gagged as he invaded my throat. I hadn't gotten a chance to take a deep breath, and I started to panic a little. Oh shit! Shit! Shit! Shit!

I tried pulling back but he held firm. His hand fisted in my hair, his big body rigid. I thought briefly about biting him to get his attention, my eyes tearing up and lungs screaming for oxygen, but before I could bite or pull his hand from my head, he was shouting and coming down my throat.

I struggled to swallow it all but was unable to keep up with the force of his orgasm, and I felt cream seep out the side of my mouth along with my saliva. When he'd shot his last drop, his hand loosened in my hair and I surged back, wincing as his fingers got caught in my hair. I sucked in a harsh breath and turned on him.

"You. Mother. Fucker!" I howled. I wiped a hand over my mouth. "Who the fuck do you think you are? You nearly choked me."

"Oh God," he panted. "I'm so sorry."

I scrambled to my seat and grabbed the door handle. *Son of a bitch, treat me like a fucking hole.* I threw open the door but he grabbed the back of my coat before I could step out.

"Danny, please, I didn't mean for that to happen."

"Bullshit."

"I swear to God. I thought I could hold it back."

I turned and glared at him. "Take your fucking hand off me or you'll be pulling back a bloody stump."

He stared at me for a moment, but he must have seen how serious I was, and dropped his hand. "Please, Danny," he pleaded as he tucked his softening dick back in his jeans and fastened them up.

"Please what?"

"I just lost it. I don't even know what to say."

"Bullshit," I repeated. "That has got to be the lamest excuse I've ever heard. You're not a goddamn preteen with a hair trigger."

"Danny—"

Whatever he was about to say was cut off when a car pulled into the lot. I blinked and shielded my eyes as its lights landed on us.

"C'mon, I'll take you home."

I slammed the door. My back was ramrod straight, arms crossed over my chest, just vibrating with pissed off. "Let's go."

"What can I do to make it up to you?" Lance asked as we pulled out of the garage.

"How about not pulling that stunt again?"

"I won't. I swear!"

Lance sounded sincere and it really wasn't that huge of a deal. Probably wouldn't have minded had I had a little bit of warning. I also think it was more the idea of Lance using me as nothing more than a hole. The idea just didn't sit right with me. Finally I was able to get my shit together enough to play it off as no big deal. I sighed and leaned my head back. "Look, I know you got carried away, I get it, but I'd really rather my obituary not read: Daniel Anderson Marshal, beloved son of Mr. and Mrs. Marshal, died unexpectedly with a dick lodged in his throat."

Lance laughed and shook his head. "Can't say as I blame you. I'll try—"

"Try?"

"Okay, okay. No more randy teenage shit. I promise." He turned to me briefly, a smirk on his face. "It's not totally my fault, you know. If you weren't so goddamn good with that pretty mouth of yours, I'd have better restraint."

"Best you'll ever have."

Lance pulled up to the dorm. "No argument there."

Now that my anger had dissipated, the memory of Lance's kiss, his hand in my hair, flavor on my tongue, my arousal began to renew. "Wanna come in for a bit?"

"I'd love to, but I have algebra homework due in the morning. Unless…."

Yeah, that wasn't going to happen. Last time he had a paper due and I offered to help, I ended up doing the homework while he laid his head in my lap, arms around my waist, and slept. *Dammit. Guess it's going to be me and my hand again.*

"Don't even think about it." I opened the door. "You're on your own this time. I got my own studying to do." I stepped out of the car.

"Hey, Danny?"

I leaned back down to meet his eyes.

"I really am sorry. Let me make it up to you by taking you to breakfast. Say seven?"

I'd have rather he made it up to me by putting his lips to my dick and relieving the ache that had settled into my sac, but that wasn't going to happen. Lance still hadn't checked off "cocksucker" on his sexual experience list yet.

"Okay. Meet you at the coffee shop?"

"Yup. See you then."

I shut the door and headed up to my room. Somehow, the night hadn't gone as I hoped. Lance got my mouth; I got my hand and a raw throat. Life just wasn't fair. At least I got a $4.99 meal out of the deal. Whoopie!

SHIT! I jerked awake, catching myself at the last second before I fell out of the chair. The last thing I'd remembered was sitting at the desk reading and… nothing. I yawned, spine cracking and popping as I stretched. I tried to focus on the open book in front of me, but it was blurry. I needed to finish this damn chapter. I hadn't done so well on the last test in my directing class and I'd be damned if I was going to have to repeat it in the spring. I was an actor, not a director.

I rubbed at my eyes and concentrated on the text until the words came into focus. I hadn't even read an entire paragraph when my cell phone rang. Concerned as to why someone was calling this late— maybe Bo was in trouble—I went to my vanity and grabbed my phone.

"Hello?"

"Where are you?"

"Uh, home studying, why?"

"You were supposed to meet me for breakfast ten minutes ago. Your coffee is getting cold."

For the first time since I'd woken, I glanced at the digital clock. Its red numbers flashed 7:11. *Ah hell.* The last time I'd checked it was just after three. I'd slept sitting at my desk for four hours.

"I'm on my way."

I ended the call and rushed to change my sweats to jeans and my T-shirt for a clean one. *Four hours? How the hell had that happened?* I could have canceled breakfast and studied, but if I didn't know it at that point, I wasn't going to, and a double shot of espresso would do more good than an hour-long cram session.

A beanie to cover my crazy knotted hair and a little Visine was the best I could do to make myself presentable. I slipped on my boots, shrugged into my wool pea coat, and stuffed my books into my satchel.

I was frazzled and frozen, but I made it to the coffee shop in record time.

I spotted Lance at the back of the shop, sitting with Bo and Katie. I hadn't expected that, but okay.

"Good morning, sleepyhead," Bo drawled as I slid into a seat next to him. "Glad to see you could join us."

"Morning, Danny," Katie chirped in, way too perky for my liking.

"This mine?" I pointed at a cup in the center of the table, grabbing it and taking a big gulp before anyone even responded. Good thing it was lukewarm. "Morning," I grumbled and took another big swig.

"I just ordered you a double shot of espresso. Lance said he had to wake you, figured you needed it."

"Thanks, you figured correctly," I said to Bo, then nodded toward Lance, who was sitting on the other side of me. "Morning."

Lance's chair was scooted close to his sister's and he was leaning toward her, as if he'd been telling her something in her ear when I showed up. He never straightened, just smiled, and said, "Good morning."

Bastard looked like he'd had a full night's sleep, his eyes bright, not a trace of the dark circles that were a telltale sign of pulling an all-nighter. His hair was also brushed, and his beard trimmed shorter than it had been when I'd seen him the night before. He looked damn good. I hated him. Appreciated how good he looked, but still hated him for being all put together and awake while I felt like a total bum and my brain still wasn't firing on all cylinders.

"Mmm hmm." I downed the rest of my coffee. Thankfully the barista—a new girl I didn't recognize—showed up and set my double espresso in front of me. She started to walk away, but I stopped her. "Hey, can I get another coffee to go?"

"Sure, what would you like?"

"Extra-large double-double, please."

"Anyone else like anything?" she asked and picked up my empty cup.

"I think we're ready to order breakfast now," Bo told her.

The three of them ordered breakfast, but I declined. I didn't have time to wait and quite honestly, my gut was a little jittery. I really needed to pass that damn exam and I wasn't feeling too confident about it.

Before the barista walked away, Lance said, "Could you add a chocolate chip muffin to his to-go order please?" He indicated me with his thumb.

As soon as she walked away, I glared at Lance. "I said I didn't want anything."

"Yeah but you will." He ignored my obvious irritation and smiled warmly.

Fucker! What was he up to?

"We should do this more often," Katie said. "I don't see you nowhere near enough these days."

"Not my fault you have your head so far up Bo's butt you can't find time for your brother."

"Okay, Mr. I-never-text-my-sister-back. I tried to get you to meet me and Bo last night, if you remember correctly, and twice last week."

"Yeah, well...." Lance snuck a quick glance in my direction. "Been a little crazy lately."

That was an understatement. He'd been a lot crazy lately.

Katie slapped Lance's arm playfully. "Yeah, then stop blaming me! At least Bo wants to spend time with me, unlike some people."

"Yeah, but I'm not trying to get in your pants."

"Lance!" She hit him again.

Bo blushed but said nothing. Really, what could he say? I had no doubt he was spending a lot of time in Katie's pants. When he wasn't in class, he was with Katie. Hell, they shared a couple of classes together, and since they were in the same business program, they often studied together. I rarely saw him, not that I had been available lately myself. When we'd been in junior high and high school, we'd rarely gone a day without seeing each other, but things had changed since arriving in Ann Arbor. Although we shared a room, we really didn't spend that much time together. We were still close, both of us knew we could depend on each other if need be, but we simply didn't run in the same circles anymore.

I sat there getting my caffeine buzz while Lance and Katie bantered back and forth playfully. A quick glance at my phone informed me I had fifteen minutes.

"So, you plan on coming home at all this week?" I asked Bo.

"Not really sure. I've got a hell of a course load and contrary to what you're thinking, Katie and I really are studying most nights."

"Mmm hmm. Well, just make sure on the few nights you're not studying, you're wrapping it before you're slapping it."

"Shh." Bo looked to Lance and Katie who were paying us no attention. "Not so loud, and I could say the same to you."

"What, you don't want her brother knowing you're boinking?" I whispered. "Your secret is safe with me. Although my guess? He already knows. And you don't concern yourself with my wrappings. I'd have to get lucky enough to need one."

"I thought you and…." He gave a curt nod in Lance's direction.

I scrunched up my face.

"Really? So you two really are just friends?"

I nodded. I hated lying to Bo, but I couldn't tell him the truth. As tempting as it was to talk about Lance with Bo, I wasn't about to be the one to out a man. That had to be his choice and on his own terms, and besides, said individual was sitting less than six feet from me and talking to his frickin' sister.

"Wow! So no one?"

"Nope," I murmured and downed the last of my espresso.

"No wonder you're so cranky lately."

"Shut up!" We both laughed and I was relieved that line of questioning was over.

The barista brought breakfast for the other three as well as my coffee and muffin to go. When I tried to pay for it, Lance stopped me. "I got his," he told her; to me, he said, "I invited you, so my treat."

"Thanks."

"Since you invited me and Bo, does that mean you're paying for ours as well?"

Okay, that caught me off guard. Why hadn't Lance mentioned he had invited them? I was under the impression this was a last-minute thing to apologize. So much for an apology. Whatever.

"No, I planned on sticking you with the bill."

"Brat!"

Lance just smiled at his sister and shoved nearly an entire biscuit in his mouth. Eww!

I grabbed my bag and coffee and stood. "Thanks again for the coffee." I held up the bag. "And the muffin. Good seeing you two. Don't be such strangers."

Bo bumped his fist against mine, nearly dislodging the bag. "See ya."

"Bye, Danny. We definitely have to do this again," Katie said with a wave.

"Sounds good."

"I'll text you later," Lance said around another big bite without looking at me.

I left the shop with my breakfast and coffee and wondered what the hell that was all about as I hurried to my class.

CHAPTER
Ten

WHEN I'd first met Lance, I'd relegated him to the dumb jock category. However, by the end of April, I was starting to think so not a jock, that it was me who was dumb. The month started okay. Weather-wise, April in Michigan sucks. Everything is starting to thaw, it rains all the damn time, and it's one big muddy, wet mess. Still, it's like the first indication that we are finally thawing and can now come out of winter hibernation, or at least had the promise of shucking our winter coats.

I hadn't seen much of Lance the last couple of weeks. In fact, our only interaction was through text—my new daily routine included a text each morning that said *Good morning cranky*—and one breakfast date. I say date, but it was like the previous breakfast meeting. Bo and Katie had been invited and I spent my time teasing Bo, and Lance spent his teasing Katie. It really shouldn't have surprised me how little Lance and I saw of each other—like Bo and his group of math nerds, Lance ran with the football jocks, neither of which held any interest for me.

Our occasional orgasmic meet-and-greets had come to a sudden halt when Katie had a falling out with her roommate, and so she and Bo had been studying and playing kissyface either in our room or down in the student lounge. Lance lived with a bunch of his jock buddies so that was a no.

The weatherman predicted unseasonably warm temps, and for once he was right. I decided, instead of running on the treadmill at the campus gym, I'd run through the park. I'm naturally thin and sexy, good genes, but that doesn't mean I don't need to keep what I got toned. Plus, running helps to clear my head.

Ear buds in, the Rolling Stones rockin' on my MP3 player, I jogged through the park. The sun was just coming up over the horizon and I had the roadway all to myself at that early morning hour. After the first mile my legs began to burn slightly, and I had to force myself to push past it. Running outdoors is a lot different from a mechanical soft surface and my thighs were reminding me of that fact.

I veered off the main road onto a dirt path that wound its way through the woods. Sweat trickled down my spine, my heart was pumping, and rock and roll blasted in my ears. My mind wandered to the upcoming show. Was I ready? Could I pull off a convincing Tony? Would I make my dad proud of my performance? As I continued to run across the darkened pathway, the pain and burn were forgotten as I began running through lines, entry points, and stage setup.

Something slammed into my back, and then an arm went around my waist and lifted me off the ground.

"What the—"

A hand clamped over my mouth and panic raced through me as I was pulled away from the path. For a split second, I froze and allowed them to take me farther into the woods. The irony of the Stones belting out "I Go Wild" in my ear was not lost on me when my brain caught up fast and I began to struggle, hands reaching back to grab at hair, feet kicking, heels connecting with shins, and doing my best to bite the hand over my mouth. My heart felt like it was going to explode out of my chest it was beating so hard with fear. In my fight to free myself from my captive, my ear bud fell from my ear and I heard a familiar voice.

"Ouch! Danny, stop, it's me." His hand fell away from my mouth the instant I stopped struggling.

"Jesus, you scared the hell out of me," I hissed. My fingers finally found purchase in his hair and I yanked hard.

"Ow!"

"Serves you right. Now put me the hell down so I can kick your ass."

"Holy fuck! You're like a little wild man." Lance chuckled and carefully set me on my feet and pried my clenched fist from his hair.

"You're lucky I couldn't get my foot up high enough or you'd be singing soprano."

Next thing I knew, I was pushed up against a wide oak tree and Lance's gorgeous gray eyes were roaming over my face, twinkling with mischief. "I have no doubt you could have done some permanent damage. You're a lot stronger than you look."

"Damn right I am."

Lance leaned in and brushed his lips against mine. "I did try to get your attention." He pulled the other bud out of my ear and kissed a path to the sensitive flesh below it. "Although I'm kind of glad you forced me to such extreme measures."

I shuddered. I hadn't been with him or anyone else, including my hand, in far, far too long, and my dick instantly responded to his nearness. I tilted my head, giving him more room to lick and suck at my neck. I grabbed his hips and pulled his groin hard against mine. He was just as aroused as I was and moaned against my neck when our cocks came in contact.

"Far too long." He echoed the words in my head.

"Not my fault," I said and shoved down his sweats, exposing his dick. I wrapped my fist around him and slowly began to slide it up and down his length. I had no idea if we could be seen if anyone ran by, but I didn't let it stop me. The thrill of getting caught only increased my desire.

Lance wasn't worried about spectators either. He shoved my shorts down, pushed my hand away, and took us both in his big hand. He set a hard and fast rhythm, his calloused fingers and palm adding to the friction and pushing me to the edge in just a few pulls.

"Not going to last long," I gritted out, hips snapping.

"Nuh uh," Lance grunted and added pressure.

I had just enough time to move my hand over our dicks to prevent us both from ending up wet when I felt the first burst of cum hit my palm. I threw my head back, slamming it against the bark, but the pain was lost to the pleasure as I shot against my hand, our combined juices flowing back over our cockheads. I clung to Lance with my free hand, my hold on him keeping me grounded through each pulse of my orgasm, then hung on to him to keep from falling when my knees threatened to buckle.

As we stood there catching our breaths, I felt Lance begin to shake, and felt his muffled laughter against my neck.

"What's so damn funny?"

"You made me break my promise." Lance stepped back, pulled up his sweats, and looked down at his wet hand. His brows furrowed in disgust and he shook his hand, dislodging most of the mess, before wiping it across his thigh.

I thought about licking my hand clean just to see the look on Lance's face. I loved shocking him. He was too damned cute with his nose all wrinkled up. Instead, I wiped my own hand on the small towel still hooked to my waistband and pulled up my shorts.

"What promise would that be? I don't remember you promising not to accost me and jerk me off in public." I pursed my lips. "I so wouldn't have let you make that one."

"You liked that, did you?"

"It was hot! Scary as hell at first, but hot. Next time I think I'll try jogging down a dark alley." I waggled my brows at him.

Lance studied my face for a moment then shook his head. "You scare me sometimes."

"Then we're even. So what promise did you break?"

"The one about being a randy teenager when I was around you. Christ, Danny, it's been two weeks and I saw your cute butt in those shorts and—" He shrugged. "Once again, all your fault."

I looked back over my shoulder briefly, trying to see my ass, and then winked at him. "You're right, my fault. However, the two-week thing is not."

We started walking back toward the still-deserted path. "I know that crap between Katie and Dani needs to get fucking resolved and fast."

"The roommate feud isn't the only problem, you know."

"Yeah, I know, but can't do anything about our schedules or living arrangements. Hey…." He stopped on the path and turned toward me. "I got to run up to Grand Blanc and pick up my phone tomorrow. Why don't you ride with me? We can stop on the way back and grab some lunch. I know a place that has the best macaroni and cheese on the planet."

I'm not sure why my gut fluttered pleasantly—maybe because it sounded like a date, but that was ridiculous. Just one friend keeping another friend company on a long ride, it had nothing to do with a date or the chance to spend the day with Lance. Nope.

"I can cut my one class, but I'd have to be back no later than five. I have dress rehearsal."

"I'll have you back in plenty of time." Lance scanned the area then leaned in and placed a chaste kiss to my lips. "I'll pick you up at ten."

"Cool."

He jogged off in the direction we had just come from. I popped my ear buds back in my ears, the Rolling Stones still playing, and started to jog in the opposite direction. *I think that boy was following me.* I smiled at the thought, but not at a date I didn't have with a guy I wasn't hot on. Nope.

I WAS just putting the final touches on my hair, bangs teased high until every bold purple strand stood perfectly from the nearly white blond base, when my cell chirped. I checked it to find a text from Lance.

Running late, grab two coffees, and I'll meet you outside the shop.

I sent back a reply. *Is it raining?*

While I waited, I added a little more shine to my lips and did my best fish lips impersonation, tilting my head from side to side to check every detail. "Honey, you look fan-fucking-fabulous!" I chuckled at myself, but it was true. The new pale purple shirt complemented the color in my hair and on my eyes and what could I say? I was gorgeous. *And conceited*, my inner party pooper reminded me, but I ignored it.

When my phone chirped again the text read *No.*

Sighing, I grabbed my coat, shoved my cell and wallet in the inside pocket, and headed out. Guess I was coffee boy this morning. I'd just made it to the door to the stairwell when Mike called out behind me.

"Hey, Danny. Wait up."

"I'm kind of in a hurry, Mike."

"Going to go meet that hot jock of yours?" he asked, his voice dripping with contempt.

My gut fell. "What hot jock?" I asked innocently, but dread was beginning to settle into my chest.

"Oh, did you two have a falling out? Is that why I haven't seen him around lately?" Mike waved a hand like he was dismissing the thought. "He wasn't your type anyway."

"If you're talking about Lance, he's just a friend. His sister is dating Bo."

"Mmm hmmm." However, I could tell from the look on Mike's face he didn't believe the lie. "Anyway, just wanted to remind you about the spring fling party this weekend, hope to see you there."

Shit! Had Mike been watching Lance come and go from my room? And if he had, who was he telling? I felt sick. Should I warn Lance about the possible rumors, or should I keep my mouth shut?

By the time I stepped out of the shop with two extra-large Styrofoam cups, Lance waiting at the curb, I'd decided I wasn't going to say anything to him. They were only rumors and Lance hadn't been hanging out at my dorm as much. They would blow over, I was sure of it. There were always new rumors starting every day, we'd just have to be more careful, was all. When I approached, he leaned over and opened the door.

"Morning, cranky." He took both the coffees, putting them in the holder. "Thanks."

"At least you didn't say 'good'," I grumbled and slid into the seat, buckling in before sucking on my burning knuckles. I appreciated the fact that they were giving me my money's worth and filling the cups to the rim, but really, I valued my flesh more than an extra sip of joe.

"You really aren't a morning person, are you?"

"I think we have already established the fact that I hate mornings. Especially mornings that have me up walking across campus and having my flesh burned from my body. All before I've had my first cup of coffee." Not to mention finding out I was at the center of rumor central. I could have cared less what they were saying about me, but if it got bad for Lance, I might not ever see him again. The thought made me physically ill. So I kept it to myself.

"Aww, poor Danny. Do you have a boo-boo you need me to kiss?"

"Shut up."

He laughed and as he drove with one hand, he reached over and grabbed my hand, gently rubbing his thumb across my knuckles. It was hard to stay cranky, even with my caffeine levels dangerously low. His smile was broad, the sound of his laughter happy, and his palm warm against mine, and I had to admit to myself he was better at putting me in a good mood than my normal morning ritual. I put all thoughts of rumors and Mike on the back burner. I'd worry about it later, maybe do some damage control, but at that moment, I was going to enjoy being with Lance.

I grabbed my coffee and blew through the small hole in the lid. "Do you have family in Grand Blanc?"

"No, just friends left. My grandparents retired to Florida last year, but growing up I spent a lot of time with them and made a lot of friends there."

"What do people in Grand Blanc do for fun?"

"A lot more than they do in Columbiaville, that's for sure."

"Like what?"

"Umm well…. They have a lot of great restaurants and they used to have a great high school football team and…." Lance tapped his thumb on the steering wheel and after a moment said, "Not really that much more than Columbiaville but they do have more people."

"Sounds like a great town," I said dryly. "Really, that's all there is to do there?"

"About it. The occasional four-wheeling, tailgate parties, hunting in the fall."

"What! No John Deere races or who-can-spit-their-chew-the-farthest contest?"

"Only on Sundays." He laughed. "Sorry we ain't as cultured as you city folks from the D."

"Obviously."

Lance looked at me over the top of his shades and I swear I saw him roll his eyes at me. "What did you do for fun growing up?"

"You saw my parents at the theater—they live for it and raised me to love it too. Dad's a performer off-Broadway and Mom was a dancer, so I grew up going to see plays, musicals, ballets, and on the rare occasion a show wasn't in town, we spent a lot of time at museums, art galleries, art fairs, stuff like that."

"What about friends?"

"I went to high school at an academy of performing arts, so most of my friends are into the same things I am."

"And what do performing arts kids do for fun when they're not being all arty?"

"You're awful nosy this morning. What's up?"

Lance maneuvered us onto the expressway heading north and set the cruise. "You started it, but now you got me curious. So...."

"There was a small group of us who hung out a lot. There was always a party, a rave to crash, something. Probably not that much different than the stuff you and your friends did."

"Crashed parties, sure. But I can honestly say my buds and I never crashed a rave."

"They aren't just for gay boys, you know," I said and frowned.

"No! I didn't mean it that way." He pointed at his face. "Can you imagine this mug in makeup? And I'm small compared to most of my friends. They would look ridiculous in drag."

"Oh, honey, you obviously have never been to a rave if you think everyone only dresses in drag. I'd love to take you sometime."

"Yeah?"

I pulled down my sunglasses and batted my lashes at him. "Oh, yeah."

"That sounds ominous."

It wasn't ominous but it would be a riot to see straight-laced Lance Lenard in the club setting. I suspected the poor guy wouldn't be able to get it up with the amount of blood that would be flushing his face in embarrassment. I was serious that raves weren't strictly for the gay boys, but for the ones I attended, the straight guys were definitely a minority. Add in alcohol and more drama queens than on a high school cheerleading team, and I'd have a ball just watching Lance squirm.

I hid my snort of laughter in my cup.

We spent the rest of the time chatting about clubs and our favorite music. Classic rock seemed to be the only thing we had in common, but for some reason I couldn't quite explain, I loved just being near him. Our conversation was light, playful, and before I knew it, we were pulling into a nice subdivision. Tree-lined streets, large brick homes, and lawns impeccably landscaped. We pulled into a driveway at the end of a cul-de-sac and I whistled low. It was the largest house in the neighborhood and the façade of the home—as well as the black Mercedes parked next to the dark green Jaguar in the driveway—screamed, "Look at me, I'm the richest on the block."

Lance put the car in park behind the Mercedes but didn't cut the engine. "I'll only be a second."

"Okay."

He'd barely made it up the walkway when a blonde came running out of the front door and threw herself at Lance. From where I sat, I could see him visibly stiffen, but I'm pretty sure it was for my benefit when the girl threw her arms around his neck, practically crawling up his body, and pressed their mouths together. From the way she behaved, this was the way they always greeted each other. And the kiss wasn't a just-friend kind, that's for damn sure.

My stomach rolled as I watch the two of them, standing not fifteen feet away from me. I gritted my teeth and forced myself to look away. I felt sick, betrayed, and trembled with anger. The rage flooding me was completely irrational. Even in the grips of jealousy, I recognized how absurd it was, but I was helpless against it. I was also powerless to keep my eyes averted.

When I looked back, Lance was hurriedly leading her to the front door by the hand. At the last minute, she turned back, our eyes met, and I turned away quickly. I recognized her as the girl Lance had brought to the theater, and the ugly green-eyed monster roared again. How long had they been dating? Did she know about Lance's secret? I highly doubted it. It was a dirty little secret, one he'd protect at all costs, and I knew that in the pit of my gut.

Get it together, man, I internally chastised myself. Lance was a jerk-off buddy, a JOB, nothing more, so why did I care who he was dating? I was sick in my gut and in my head. I was turning into a total nut job, arguing with myself, trying to tell that part of me that was screaming *you're falling in love with him* to shut the fuck up, when the driver-side door opened and Lance slid into the car.

On the inside was this crazy torrent of emotions, like two sides of me were literally battling it out, slashing and tearing away at each other, leaving me dizzy and nauseated. But I hid it. I would not let Lance know what that kiss did to me. I plastered on a fake smile and asked, "Get your phone?"

"Yeah."

He pulled out of the drive without sparing a look my way. I could tell he was still tense, perhaps waiting for an attack, at least a verbal one. He wouldn't get it. Although inside the battle of raging storm of emotions continued, on the outside I was completely calm and at ease. I was an actor and damn good at becoming someone else, and as we drove back south, I was Mr. Happy-go-lucky without a care in the world.

It was a great performance.

CHapTer
eLeven

THE Unity sat right smack dab in the center of Main Street. An old church built in the 1840s, it had long been converted into a restaurant. I was all smiles when I held the door open for Lance.

"After you, sir."

He gave me a skeptical look, but he allowed me to hold the door for him. As I stepped inside, the scent of smoked meats and spices filled my nostrils, and my stomach growled, reminding me I hadn't eaten. The décor had an authentic feel to the building's original purpose. Oak floors, large stained glass windows that lit up the room in vibrant colors, even the pews that were used instead of booths looked as if they'd been available during Sunday morning sermons when the church first opened its doors.

In the center of the room, more pews sat back to back with several tables placed in front of them, running the length of the restaurant, and a wooden bar spanned the entire back wall. I couldn't help but snicker when "*now that would make church way more interesting*" popped into my head.

We seated ourselves at one of the booths—pews—and I grabbed a menu from the rack. "This place is so cool. What do you recommend?"

Lance pushed his shades up on his head; his eyes still looked wary. He could wait all he wanted. I was not going to ask him about the peppy blonde girlfriend. I gave him a big ol' smile. "Well? You have been here before, haven't you?"

He nodded. "They are known for their sausage, and the macaroni and cheese brings people from all over."

I set the menu aside. "Then I'll have both."

I looked up just as a waiter set water glasses down in front of us. "Hi, I'm Bran. Welcome to the Unity, have you ever dined with us before?"

Bran was tall, lean, with a well-toned body, head full of shaggy brown hair, and dark stubble on his jaw. His smile was warm with just enough of a smirk to make it sassy. I couldn't help but think that by the way he was looking at me, he was used to seeing men in full makeup, or he simply liked it, since there wasn't a shred of disgust evident in his eyes, nor was there shock or confusion. And there was no denying the attraction in those baby blues. I liked him instantly. He had good taste and he was frickin' hot.

I shifted to give Bran my full attention. "My friend here has, but it's my first time. What do you recommend?" It was irrelevant that I'd already decided what I would be having.

"The pecan and cherry-smoked pork sausage with sautéed mushrooms and onions is really good. Sandwich-wise I'd recommend the Panino, and of course, our mac and cheese is very good."

I rested my elbow on the table, chin cradled in my palm, and looked up at him through my lashes. "What's on the Panino?" I asked in full flirt mode.

"Salami, pepperoni, capicola, provolone, lettuce, tomato, and vinaigrette on a baguette. It comes with our house potato salad."

"Mmmm, sounds yummy, I'll have that and the macaroni and cheese, and water is fine."

"Great choice." Bran turned his attention to Lance, who was now scowling. "Do you know what you're going to have or would you like a few more moments?"

"Large mac and cheese with ham and a Coke."

"I'll get those in for you right away."

Bran walked down the aisle and my eyes were instantly drawn to his cute butt. The plaid shorts he wore hugged the tight globes, giving a glimpse of the flexing muscles as he moved. Holy Jesus, he had the most amazing wiggle I'd ever seen. Being an ass man, I'd checked out a lot of asses in my life and never had I seen anyone who swayed and moved as he did. It was pure boner-popping perfection.

"See something you like?"

Without looking away from that mesmerizing walk, I answered, "Mmm hmm. That boy would be fucking amazing in heels. He has nailed the sexy walk."

"Danny, he has a beard," Lance bit out.

His angry tone grabbed my attention. I smiled, and with exaggerated sugary sweetness, said, "Oh, honey, I noticed. He's all man beneath that diva strut, but he'd still look damn good in heels, beard and all. However, there is this little thing men have been using for ages called a razor if he decided to do full-on drag. Although, you seem to have forgotten how to use it as of late."

Lance pursed his lips, his face flushed, and I swear I could see him vibrating. "I thought you liked the beard."

"I do. But, unlike you, I like variety in my men. A tiny twink can be just as entertaining and sexy as a big hairy bear. Not that Bran is in either of those categories. That man is in a class of his own."

Yes, I was baiting him. My sarcasm tends to get downright bitchy when I'm irritated. I wasn't lying about our waiter, he really was sexy, in an adorable, snuggle-you kind of way. And normally, I would have kept those thoughts to myself around a date. However, after witnessing what I had earlier, I was hurt, and I refused to define our shared lunch as a date. My defense mechanism in hiding my pain is my wit and it burst forth in the form of acrimony.

Bran showed up with Lance's Coke. I was proud of Lance for not snapping at his hand when he set the glass down in front of him, but I'm pretty sure he was thinking about it with the grunt of "thank you" that sounded very much like a growl.

"Your meals will be out shortly," Bran said.

Bless his heart, Bran was a smart man. He knew exactly what I was doing, as evidenced by the way he glanced at a brooding Lance and gave me a wink before he left to work his strut and I purposely leaned to watch the show.

Neither of us said a word to each other as we waited for our lunch. I occupied myself with watching the people around us as they dined, while Lance sat across from me, both hands clutching his glass, scowling at the dark-colored liquid as if he was mad at it for not being something stronger. I knew exactly whom he was mad at but continued to ignore him.

The silence continued until a plate of bubbling-over-the-sides mac and cheese was set in front of me. The first bite of cheese-strewn noodle had me practically moaning in delight. "Oh my God, this is so good."

"Told ya," Lance responded curtly without looking up from his lunch. "Better than the company."

"What the hell is that supposed to mean?"

His head snapped up and he glared at me. "You're being fucking rude and you know it," he hissed.

"How so? I think I'm being very nice, sickly sweet even."

"Never mind."

I shrugged nonchalantly as if I couldn't care less what he thought and dug into my lunch; both items Bran had suggested were amazing.

I was doing very well with the nasty looks Lance was giving me, responding to each one with a wide grin. But I admit, I probably—okay, I did—take it too far when Bran came to take our empty plates.

"Would either of you like dessert? May I suggest the caramel-glazed custard. It's decadent, especially with a Bailey's and coffee."

"I'm stuffed, and I have to pass on the drink until Saturday?"

"Saving yourself for a big party?"

"More like waiting till I turn twenty-one."

"It's your birthday Saturday? Why didn't I know this?" Lance grumbled.

"You didn't ask," I said dryly.

"Happy early Birthday. I work at the Scarlet Romeo on the weekends. Marilyn Mon'Rod does a fantastic rendition of Happy Birthday; you should stop by."

Lance snorted.

"Thanks for the invite. I may just take you up on it."

Bran set the bill down on the table and I snatched it up before Lance could. "I invited you for lunch," he complained, holding out his hand for the bill.

"Yes, but I'm paying for the entertaining company you've provided." It was a low blow but I knew he hadn't enjoyed his lunch and I didn't want to feel obligated to him in any way simply because he'd paid for lunch.

When Bran returned to the table, he handed me the leather case. "Thank you, Mr. Marshal."

"Danny, please." I held out my hand.

"Danny," Bran echoed and shook my hand. "Nice meeting you too," he said to Lance and strutted away.

I signed the first copy and took the copy beneath with Bran's phone number. I tucked it and the receipt in my wallet with my credit card. "Ready?"

I had to rush to catch up with Lance when he jumped up and headed to the door.

As soon as we were in the car and on our way back to Ann Arbor, Lance's brooding silence finally broke. "Do you want to tell me what the fuck all that was about?"

"What are you—"

"Cut the innocent bullshit, Danny. You sat across from me with a smirk on your face and flirted with the waiter right in front of me."

"And?"

Lance slammed his hand down on the steering wheel. "And it was fucking rude."

"Tsk, tsk, tsk." I shook a finger at him. "First of all, we are friends and occasional jerk-off buddies, nothing more. So I don't find what I did any more rude than you playing tonsil hockey with some blonde little suburbanite in front of me."

"Is that what all this is about? Payback?"

Was it? Yeah, it was at first, but after thinking about it for a bit, I realized how foolish it was to be jealous or how ridiculous Lance's response to my flirting was. Lance was simply curious. Sure, we were attracted to each other, liked what we did behind closed doors, and I had no doubt he would continue to be a JOB, but never any more than that. Even if he wanted to, Lance just wasn't the kind of guy who would ever truly be comfortable with people knowing he was sexing it up with a dude. This was my issue, my fault that I'd allowed myself to fall for him and the impossible.

"Look. I admit I started out a little pissy after seeing you with her, but honestly, I realize just how stupid that is. I had no right to be pissy and I apologize for that."

"And are you're going to apologize for flirting with that guy?"

"No!" I said adamantly.

"Why the hell not?"

"Because he was cute and that's how I behave when I see an attractive man, especially one who also seems to be attracted to me. I may not have a right to be pissy about who you are seeing, but you also have no right to get upset about who I flirt with, or who I date, for that matter."

After a long period of silence, Lance finally said, "I don't like it."

"You don't have to. We are not committed to each other, hell, Lance, we rarely hang out beyond getting together once in a while to get a nut. If we were actually dating, it would be different, but we're not."

His brows furrowed, but he didn't respond.

I felt totally uncomfortable for the rest of the ride back to campus. Lance never said another word on the subject, or any other subject. He kept his eyes steadily on the road, tapping his thumbs on the steering wheel occasionally to the beat on the radio.

In one respect, I was glad we had our boundaries set, but I had this nettling feeling that there was more to his story with the girl than I knew. I was dying to ask him what their story or history was, but after I'd just told him it was none of his business who I dated, I'd sound like a hypocrite asking him about who he was seeing. I was still dying to know, since it would bother me to know they were in a serious relationship and he was cheating on her.

I rested my head against the window and stared out, seeing nothing at all, the prickling feeling of wrongness riding me hard. It's one thing to be experimental, curious, or whatever it was Lance was doing with me. I'd had the fantasy once or twice before meeting Lance about being with a straight guy, and being Lance's first experience was an ego boost. Yeah, at times it was frustrating, but it was also hot.

However, I wasn't comfortable with being the one he was cheating with. In fact, I was thinking it was time to find a new benefits buddy.

My chest tightened when I thought of not seeing Lance again, not being able to touch him…. Christ, I was falling for him, or had fallen for him, and that was so not a good thing.

Time to walk away.

By the time Lance pulled up in front of the dorm, I pretty much had myself convinced that I wouldn't see him anymore other than when we were pushed together by Bo and Katie. Only my heart seemed to be struggling with the decision, but it was definitely outnumbered.

"Thanks for asking me to ride with you. Lunch was delicious."

"You're welcome."

I hesitated, but really, there was nothing left to say. I opened the door.

"Are you going Saturday?"

"I don't know yet, why?"

"Just curious. I'll see you around?"

It wasn't a statement—he was asking. Lance looked miserable, his eyes sad as he looked at me expectantly. It was as if he'd been reading my thoughts and knew what was about to happen. I honestly didn't know if the sadness was because he'd miss me or because he knew his chapter in the book of *The Straight Boy's Guide to Fun Gay Sex* was over, at least with this guy.

For me it was a little of both. "Sure, Lance. Talk to you later."

CHaPTer
Twelve

THE smell of diesel fuel and the constant blaring of horns were making my head throb. Standing out front of the departing passenger drop-off at Detroit Metropolitan Airport wasn't how I planned on spending the morning of my twenty-first birthday. Unlike most parents, who retire and move to the Sunshine State, mine were retiring to the theater district in New York City. Instead of peace and quiet, sipping fancy drinks with colorful little umbrellas on the beach, they had chosen harsh winters, crowded streets, and constant noise. But at least they would be within walking distance of the theater. I just wished it hadn't been the day of my birthday that they booked their flight for.

I had always envisioned a champagne toast at midnight, dancing, picking up the hottest man in the club, and celebrating my birthday properly all night, all morning, and well into the early afternoon. Twenty-one is a milestone. I deserved to be waking up naked and in bed with a sexy stranger. Dammit, I should have at least had a hangover, hoarse voice from singing, and aching muscles from dancing. But, no! I had to drive to my parents' house for a quiet dinner and turn in early so I could get up at 4:00 a.m. and drive them to the airport.

I looked upward at the dark sky. *Why do you hate me?*

"Thanks again, honey," Mom said and hugged me again. "I know this isn't how you planned on spending your birthday, but I promise we'll make it up to you next month."

I felt a twinge of guilt. They did so much, bent over backwards to be there for me, and here I was whining because I didn't get laid last night. "It was a great way to spend my birthday." I kissed her cheek and hugged her back. "Love you. Thanks again for the tickets."

"You're welcome." Mom released me and grabbed her carryon bag from the curb. "Careful driving back. We'll call you when we land."

"Always am." I winked at her.

Dad came around from the back of the car where he'd been pulling out their luggage and setting it on the curb for the porter to take. "Happy Birthday, son. Love you." He pulled me into an embrace and slapped me on the back. "Thanks for the ride."

"Anytime. Love you too."

He pointed at me as he joined Mom. "You be careful tonight. If you get drunk, call a cab."

I nodded and waved as I slid back into the car. I did plan on drinking tonight, but with any luck I wouldn't be needing a cab. The vultures at the airport were watching for a space to park, and the instant I was behind the wheel, the guy in the car behind me laid on his horn. I waved again at my parents, flipped the guy off behind me just to make myself feel better, and pulled away from the curb.

While I was sitting at the first stop sign, my phone chirped. It was a message from Lance. *Happy Birthday.*

I replied with a simple *Thanks.*

I miss you.

I ignored that text. I missed him too, but I wasn't going to tell him that. I hadn't liked the feelings that had come over me when I'd seen him with that girl. In that moment I realized that I was starting to fall for Lance, and I simply couldn't afford to fall any further. I forced my thoughts away from Lance. I had to rush back, meet Lee and Cameron for brunch, nap, and then I could get ready for the real Danny Marshal Birthday Bash.

"FOR the last time, no!"

"C'mon, Danny, it will be fun." Bo's voice was pleading through the speakerphone.

He'd been trying since the day before to get me to go to some club with him and Katie for my birthday, drinks and dinner on them. While I love Bo and Katie is a great girl, my idea of hanging with the two of them at some piano bar was not how I wanted to spend my birthday. I wanted to dance and grind. I planned on dressing to the T, drinking, hooting, hollering, and flirting my ever-lovin' ass off, and it sure as hell wouldn't be in a piano bar. The most decadent dinner or offers of unlimited free drinks in a straight club would not deter me. I was going to Scarlet Romeo and I doubted I'd be buying a single drink.

"Fun for who?" I asked as I carefully attached the second set of false lashes against my lid. I batted my eyes, admiring my work in the mirror. *Gorgeous.*

"For all of us. It's not just a piano bar. They have dueling pianos and Katie said they are funny and very talented."

"No."

"I thought you liked that kind of stuff?"

"I do," I said, adding a little more mascara to my lower lashes. "Just not tonight. Tonight I plan on getting laid and I'm pretty sure I'll have a better chance of that happening at the Scarlet Romeo."

Bo huffed out a breath. "You're such a slut."

"Says the man who has a steady itch reliever," I laughed.

"Do not let Katie hear you call her that, she will flip the fuck out."

"Yeah, yeah, yeah. I gotta go, it's a little difficult to chat and put on lip liner. We'll do something tomorrow, just not too early, okay?"

"All right. Just be safe tonight."

"Will do. Don't wait up."

I started to hit the End button when Bo added, "Hey, almost forgot to ask. What was it your parents got you?"

"Dude, they are taking me to see *Chicago* while we're in New York."

"Haven't you seen it like a thousand times?"

"Not at the Ambassador Theatre. Broadway, baby!"

"And you call me a nerd." He chuckled. "Happy Birthday, Danny."

"Thanks. See you tomorrow."

My hair and face perfection, I finished dressing. When I said I planned to dress to the T, I meant it. However, that doesn't mean I was wearing anything particularly fancy or flashy. The T in this case was all about the Touch! Easy access. Low-riding jeans with a canvas belt to keep them sitting precariously on my hips, but plenty of room for fingers to brush below the waistband. I chose a black snap-up, western-style shirt with short sleeves—one good pull, and full chest exposure, baby. Six-inch heeled ankle boots, black leather and silver bracelets, and a simple leather cord necklace with a silver medallion, and I was ready.

THE Scarlet Romeo was packed when I arrived. I had to pull into a lot two blocks from the club and walk, but not even that little inconvenience could darken my mood. I was walking on cloud nine.

"ID."

I handed the bouncer my shiny new driver's license the state sent me for my special day. When you're under twenty-one, the ID reads the long way, but when you become of legal age, you get the big boy card.

He looked up at me and back down at the card. There was no mistaking that sexy hair, it was definitely me. He handed me back the license and smiled. "Happy Birthday, Mr. Marshal. Enjoy yourself."

"Oh, I plan on it." I shoved the card in my back pocket. "And thanks." I winked at him as he held the rope back, allowing me to enter the club.

The décor in the club looked how I imagine a showgirl's dressing room would look like—feather boas, sparkly accents, and drapes of billowy chiffon in soft pinks. On either side of the stage, go-go boys were up on Greek stone pedestals, dressed in white pirate shirts tied to show off their muscular stomachs, black G-strings and knee-high boots. The small tables that were scattered around the dance floor had adorable vanity chairs with scrolling ironwork and hot-pink, padded cushions.

I made my way to the bar, weaving in and out of the crowds, hands landing on my ass, eyes wandering down my body, one dude bold enough to press his palm against my crotch when I tried to squeeze between him and his friend.

"Nice," he murmured. "Buy you a drink?"

My eyes roamed down his body appreciatively. His T-shirt stretched tight across bulging pecs, leading the eye down to his thin waist and impressive bulge straining against the front of his jeans. When my gaze moved up to his, the look in his brown eyes was a blatant invitation to look all I wanted, touch if I had the mind to. And I did have mind to. No sense burning any bridges—I may need to climb back across this one. I ran my finger down his chest from breastbone to navel and said seductively, "I'm meeting a friend. Maybe later."

I moved on, the crowd swallowing me up before I could hear his response. I made it to the bar, my body vibrating with the raw sexual scent in the air. I'd been pressed against, touched, propositioned, and fondled enough that by the time I squeezed into a stool, I had to adjust my growing arousal. I ordered a Miller Lite on tap, figuring I'd start out slow and work my way up to the stronger stuff.

I sipped at my beer, turning the stool to check out the activities around me. The blaring techno music beat in time to the flashing disco balls that hung from the ceiling. There was a nice mix among the partygoers—everyone was represented, including glamorous drag queens, young college frat boys, twinks, bears, leather daddies, men in business suits, and still others in everyday jeans and T. It was like a smorgasbord of carnal delights and I was starving.

I turned my head to the right and spotted a server in black spiked heels attached to long shapely legs, tiny little ruffled denim skirt that was high enough to show a perfectly sculpted ass, and white fishnet shirt. What grabbed my attention was that ass. I would recognize that perfect butt wiggle anywhere. Bran set down a round of drinks at one of the tables, bending at the waist, putting that awe-inspiring backside on display.

He and I had talked a couple of times earlier in the week and shared numerous text messages. He was expecting me tonight and planned to introduce me to his friends. Bran was in a relationship with an author who was big and beefy. Rick looked more like a bodybuilder or physical trainer rather than a gay romance novelist, but like Bran had said, he would have been an idiot to pass up that combination of brains and brawn. While Bran may not have been available, he knew plenty of men who were single and looking for the same kind of uncomplicated relationship I was.

I knew the moment Bran spotted me; his smile grew and he practically ran in those stripper heels to give me my first lipstick mark of the night.

"You made it. Oh. My. God. You look stunning!"

"Nowhere near as fabulous as you look. The minute I saw you walk, I knew you could work a pair of stilettos like no one's business."

Bran lifted one leg and did a little graceful kick, showing off his shoes. "It's all in the size thirteens, baby." His voice was singsong and teasing.

"Thirteen?" I parroted. I fanned myself and gave him a saucy grin. "That man of yours is very, very lucky if the old wives' tales are true."

"They are, and he is." Bran winked at me and I snickered. "I gotta grab this next round for table six, but I'll be back."

"Take your time. I think I may go play on the dance floor for a bit before the show starts."

"Okay. I have a break coming in about thirty minutes, so go play, mingle, and then I'll introduce you to some of the other boys and girls." Bran leaned over and gave me a mock peck on the cheek, then strutted off to work the crowd.

I lifted my mug and took long pulls as I watched the bodies swaying on the dance floor to the upbeat music. I was itching to join them, so many men grinding and thrusting sent a buzz of arousal through me. I shifted on my stool—my jeans suddenly felt too tight, as did my skin. I downed the last of my beer, set the mug aside, and headed for the dance floor.

The lighted dance floor flashed an array of colors in time to the bass-heavy techno music, the occupants causing it to vibrate with their movements. I stepped on to it and it was like heaven beneath my feet. The air was thicker here, the smell of musk, sweat, and arousal palpable. I inhaled the enticing scent deeply, taking it in to me and let the crowd take me.

As I mentioned, I have two left feet and can't dance for shit. However, standing in the center of a crowded dance floor, bodies packed tightly together, barely enough room to do more than sway as hands roamed over bodies, it was more like foreplay than dancing. I'm really good at foreplay.

I closed my eyes as the music filled me, raised my hands over my head, and gyrated to the beat. Foreign hands roamed down my back; my flesh tingled in response to the touch, which moved downward to cup and massage my ass. More fingertips brushed along my jaw, tracing the tendons down the side of my neck. Still others caressed my chest, stomach, and groin until I became part of the rhythm. I was the music, no longer one physical body, but part of the flowing melody of arms, legs, and torsos.

The song ended, a hush falling over the club. I opened my eyes and my breath caught when I found steel-gray eyes staring at me from within the crowd. The stage lights came on and the crowd shifted and they were gone. It was only a split second, but I could have sworn Lance had been there. I knew it was ridiculous, but…. I brushed off the eerie feeling and moved with the mob off the lighted floor as a husky and sensual voice flowed from the speakers. "Good evening, boys and girls. Welcome to Scarlet Romeo."

Chapter
Thirteen

SWEAT trickled down my spine, my legs a little shaky as I moved away from the dance floor. I spotted Bran waving me over to a table. He was sitting on the lap of a large man with wavy dark brown hair and trimmed beard. I recognized him from the pictures Bran had sent me of him and his boyfriend, Rick.

Bran motioned toward the chair next to him. "Sit! I ordered you a beer."

I gratefully took the chair and the offered beer. "You're a lifesaver." I took a long pull from the brew, the cold liquid easing my dry throat.

"Everyone, this is Danny." I shook the hand Rick offered me as we both greeted each other. Bran then pointed to a broad-shouldered man with chestnut hair, his emerald T-shirt matched the green of his eyes. "That's Kegan." Kegan raised his glass in a salute toward me and smiled. I waved back. Bran then leaned close and said quietly for my ears only, "He's single, twenty-eight, hell of a nice guy, and total power bottom."

I covered my mouth discreetly with my hand and said, "Sign me up for one of those."

Bran gave me a saucy look and nodded. He then pointed to the final member of the group, a gorgeous specimen of All-American USDA choice farm boy. "That's Drake."

Drake smiled, showing off perfectly straight white teeth, the hunger in his hazel eyes unmistakable, and I squirmed in my seat as he held me in his sights. I couldn't break away from his mesmerizing stare, even when Bran leaned over and whispered. "Single, twenty-five, and don't let those boy-next-door looks fool you. He's an aggressive, kinky toppy top, but trust me, those sore muscles and bruises come morning are so fucking worth it."

As if Drake knew what Bran was saying, he winked, an amused, self-assured smile curling his lips. I swallowed hard, a jolt of lust hitting me dead center in the chest and racing south.

"Oh dear God. I'll take a helping of that too."

Bran chuckled and gave me a challenging look. "You wouldn't survive a night with the both of them."

The crowd around us went crazy. Catcalls, applause, and whistles so loud they drowned out the music, making any response I said out loud impossible to hear, but I still mouthed, "What a way to go." I took another big gulp from my beer and turned toward the stage. If the two men Bran had chosen to sit at the table with us were any indication how hot the night was going to be, I was in for a scorcher.

A tall and slender drag queen with chocolate-brown skin and a mass of wild black curls slinked across the stage. Her hips moved to the music as she worked the stage; the white, sequined material of her slinky dress caught the light and made the fabric come alive with sparkling color.

The Donna Summer lookalike did an impressive lip-synced version of "Hot Stuff," working the crowd up into a frenzy each time the phrase *"Lookin' for some hot stuff, baby, this evenin'"* came through the speakers. Men screamed "Me!" along with other more lewd suggestion on what they'd give her that evening. It was all in good fun and I was having a ball.

After Donna stepped off the stage, Bran had to go back to work, but sent over what would be the first of many rounds of beer and shots of tequila for the four of us remaining. I clapped and drank through a spicy and sexy Gloria Estefan impersonator doing "Turn the Beat Around," and after that a spectacular rendition of "The Shoop Shoop Song" by the most stunning Cher—including the diva herself—that I'd ever seen.

As the applause died down after the last performer, a debonair-looking gentleman with salt-and-pepper gray hair and a black tux made his way to the center of the stage. I eyed the shot of tequila sitting in front of me, debating whether I should throw it back or not. My head was already swimming a little and I couldn't stop giggling, a sure sign that I had moved past tipsy and was racing toward sloppy drunk. I decided against another shot. I needed to pace myself and gave my attention back to the gentleman on the stage.

"This next lady really needs no introduction," the MC crooned into the microphone. "But I will give her one anyway." He nodded to someone to the right of the stage before continuing, but his speech was lost on me when the two go-go boys I'd seen dancing on pedestals earlier came and stood on either side of me.

"Danny," the one standing on my right said, and held out his hand. "Would you come with us, please."

I shot a look to my companions in confusion, but the three of them were all smiles and waved me on. I shrugged. "What the hell." As long as they didn't expect me to show off any fancy dance moves or do too much spinning, I was game.

I placed my hand in Sexy Go-Go Boy Number One's hand and allowed him to help me to my feet. I swayed a little as the room spun and gripped his hand tighter to steady myself. Go-Go Boy Number Two, bless his heart, hooked his arm in mine, and the two of them led me to a chair that had been set in the center of the dance floor facing the stage.

"Thank you, boys," I slurred as they guided me to sit. They then each leaned down, gave me a kiss on the cheek, and wished me a happy birthday. I thanked them by patting each of their tight little buns as they moved back toward the stage. The crowd around me went nuts, screaming, and clapping. I looked up to see the source of their frenzied applause. Stepping out onto the stage in a calf-length, snow-white fur coat, six-inch white stiletto heels, and a head full of platinum blonde waves was none other than Marilyn Monroe—I mean, Marilyn Mon'Rod—herself.

She stepped up to the microphone, clutching her coat to her chest, a sensual smile curling her bright red-painted lips. When she sighed huskily into the mic and dropped her coat to expose the white halter dress with classic flowing pleats, the crowd went wild again. I gotta say, the cleavage on Marilyn Mon'Rod was as impressive as her long shapely legs. But to my astonishment, she went one better and began to sing. Not lip-syncing like the other performers relied on, but actually singing, and her voice was beautiful as she began to belt out "Happy Birthday, Mr. Marshal."

Marilyn never took her eyes from me as she slithered and pranced across the stage to the stairs, where Go-Go Dancer One and Go-Go Dancer Two held out their hands to help her gracefully swish and sway down each step.

I was held captivated by the glamorous and sexy vixen as she made her way to me, singing a cappella. Not a single noise from the club interrupted her, not the clink of ice in a glass, a cough, nothing while the entire club was held under her spell, and lucky me, she was heading my way.

Marilyn stood before me, the tone of her voice pure as she came to the end of the song. She then swung one long shapely leg across my lap, straddled me, and whispered, "Happy Birthday to you," close to my ear. She placed a big wet one on my smiling face then hopped off my lap and blew kisses to the roaring crowd.

"C'mon, everyone! Come wish the birthday boy the best birthday ever."

The crowd surged around us as the DJ blasted a new dance mix through the speakers. I was kissed, patted on the back, and hugged too many times to count, and I have to admit, it was the best birthday to date.

As the song morphed into something softer, large arms wrapped around me from behind. "Can I have this dance?"

I turned in Drake's arms, reached up, and placed my hands on his shoulders. "I would love to."

Drake pulled me in closer, molding our bodies together, one of his legs sliding between my thighs and pressing against my groin as we rocked to the music. I inhaled deeply—his scent was a little sweaty, a little spicy, and reminded me of the cologne Lance wore. Even as my heart began to pound, my dick filling at Drake's nearness, I couldn't help but wish it were Lance's muscular body against mine and his strong arms wrapped around me.

"Having a good time?" he asked, having to shout to be heard over the crowd and the music.

"Amazing!" And I was, despite the longing that caused a slight ache in my chest.

Talking was nearly impossible so I laid my head on his chest as he slowly and rhythmically controlled the dance. So many couples shared the floor with us, still more sitting at tables or standing near the bar with their heads close in conversation.

Each circular pass, my attention kept landing on one couple in particular. The dark-haired man, who looked to be middle-aged, lines around his eyes and silver strands in his hair, had his arm wrapped around his blond companion's shoulders. There was a familiarity between them that made me think these two men hadn't just met, but were lovers. As the dark-haired man chatted with two other guys sitting across from him, he stroked blond guy's chest, who was looking up at him with what I could only describe as wonderment. I had seen that same kind of look on Lance's face when I'd woken in his arms and found him watching me sleep.

In fact, I'd seen that expression on Lance's face many times when I'd catch him staring at me. Did he feel something more for me? While lying against each other playing solitaire on the laptop, hadn't Lance draped his arm around me and absently stroked my flesh much as the dark-haired man was doing now? My heart began to pound faster. The little things he did. Sending me text messages in the middle of the night so I'd awaken to *Good Morning, Cranky*, which never failed to make me smile. Knowing me well enough to order a muffin to go, because he knew I hadn't eaten and wouldn't get a chance to.

Ah, Christ! On the dance floor, wrapped in another man's arms, I realized I'd fallen for the big, sweet jock. I had warned myself against it, that Lance would never be more than a JOB, and I'd get my heart broken if I allowed myself to fall for him. As I stared at the couple, I realized that I wished it were Lance and me sitting there.

Heartbreak, what a stupid thing to waste a birthday wish on.

Drake's hand slid down and back from my waist to squeeze my left ass cheek, forcing us that much closer and bringing me out of my depressing thoughts. The impressive package he was hiding in his jeans, hard against my hip, was what I should be wishing for. Carnal delights that brought pleasurable pain, not the emotional kind that could rip a heart out of a chest. I was crazy to be in a club with all these available men—hell, one grinding his hard cock against me—and thinking about an unavailable one.

Lance was probably somewhere at that very moment with his arm draped over some little bubbly blonde, laughing and drinking with his muscle-head teammates. Absently stroking a big-tittied chest, showing off to his buds what a macho manly jock he was by feeling up the captain of the cheerleading squad while I was obsessing over him again.

Oh. Hell. No! I'd show him how a *real* man had a good time.

The song ended and a faster mix began. I went up on my tiptoes to get closer to Drake's ear so I wouldn't have to shout over the music, and said, "I'm going to use the restroom. Why don't you order us a drink, and when I get back, you can tell me all about this kink I've heard so much about." I then licked his ear, making him shudder.

It took me nearly thirty minutes to work my way through the thick crowd, made all the more difficult by the sheer number of people congratulating me and numerous propositions for a good time. A couple of men offered me their *package*, claiming it to be the gift that kept giving and giving. That one made me chuckle at just how lame the come-on line was. After my time with Marilyn Mon'Rod, I was the star of the night and wouldn't be without companionship for long. All I had to do was pick and choose. Did I go with one of the many anonymous faces in the crowd and take my chances, or did I pick what was behind door number two and entertain power bottom Kegan. Still another option was deviant Dom Drake.

By the time I made it back to the table, Drake was standing there, two glasses of dark amber liquid in his hand and an oh-so-naughty smile on his face. My eyes leisurely roamed down that big body, he was all powerhouse and animal magnetism. Even his hands looked powerful, and I could imagine those blunt fingers holding on to my hips, leaving five perfectly round bruises on each one, rather than the delicate glass they were currently wrapped around. I refused to think of the dark marks Lance liked to leave on me. I sucked in my bottom lip and looked up at Drake from under my long lashes, giving him a flirty smile. My thumbs were hooked in the loops of my jeans, hands framing my interest, and when Drake's gaze landed on my crotch, I saw him take in a sharp intake of breath and lick his lips. When he looked back up and met my eyes, the lust was clearly visible. It was my turn to shudder beneath that hungry stare.

Yeah, option number three seemed like just the thing I needed for what ailed me. Drake could no doubt help me with two little problems I had. One, I hadn't been laid in way longer than any eager man in his twenties should have to endure. And two, I was betting he was more than capable of fucking all thoughts of Lance Lenard right out of my head.

AS I lay on the bar, shirt pulled open and away from my body, a tangy flavor filled my mouth as a warm, swirling tongue licked down from breastbone to navel. I held perfectly still, fighting the urge to squirm as the tickling sensation intensified as the wet, greedy mouth moved down the trail of light hair leading to my groin. My teeth clenched tighter, the acerbic juice pooling in the back of my throat, as the heavy bulge in my jeans was nuzzled. I watched as the newest partaker threw his head back, lips sealed tightly around the shot glass he'd retrieved from between my thighs, throat working as he swallowed down the clear fluid. The crowd cheered his success, then hooted and whistled when he leaned down and took my mouth, retrieving the lime wedge from between my lips.

I licked the bitter nectar from the corner of my mouth and then yelled, "Next!"

I'd spent the last hour as the Scarlet Romeo's very profitable marketing tool for Jose Cuervo. Looking around at the men still waiting for their turn at a Danny Marshal body shot, I could tell the club's tequila sales were going to be off the charts. Bran walked up with a black sleep mask dangling from his fingertips. "Someone wants a special drink."

I studied the silky material and arched a brow at Bran. "Kinky!"

He laid the mask over my eyes and I lifted my head. "This was not my idea," he whispered as he secured the elastic in place and I was in complete darkness.

I smiled, knowing exactly who would want me blindfolded. Looked like Drake was going for seconds.

With the loss of sight, my other senses seemed to become more acute. I could hear the gurgling of liquid as it was poured, and whispered voices mingling with the loud music. I could smell the strong aroma of liquor and the citrus of limes in the air. I jumped when something wet ran down the side of my neck, felt the granules of salt, coarse against my flesh.

I vibrated with the keen sensations and my shaft swelled further when a warm breath just below my ear caused my flesh to heat to a feverish level. I was suddenly, painfully hard, my cock pressed against my stomach, trapped in its denim confines, and I squirmed, trying to relieve the ache.

A shiver of recognition trickled down my spine when the spot where Lance used to mark me was licked, sharp teeth scraping over the area, then was briefly sucked. His face flashed behind my shielded eyes, stealing my breath. Why couldn't I let him go? The mouth moved away from my neck, kissed and licked across my chest, and I tried my damndest to push the images away, only I couldn't. I could smell him in the air, the touch against my hip felt familiar, and his face only solidified further in my mind.

I needed a break. A break and a drink—lots of hard, powerful drinks. I was fucking losing it.

I readied myself for what was to come, muscles tensing, preparing to flee the minute the shot was taken from my thighs and the lime removed from my mouth. The person above me stopped, however, he didn't nuzzle my groin or take the tequila. I felt the air around me cool as he backed off, taking with him his heat.

I reached up to remove the blindfold, when my wrist was grabbed in a firm grip, the lime abruptly pulled from beneath my teeth, and when I started to protest, I was silenced by a tongue thrusting deeply into my mouth. Unable to see, my hands restrained, and a foreign mouth invading mine, I became extraordinarily upset, and as the feeling reached a crescendo, I went berserk. I arched my back hard, feet kicking out as I tried to roll to dislodge my captor. His tongue slid out of my mouth before I could take a bite of the slippery invader, and then the mask was ripped away.

I blinked at the bright light, and my heart stopped beating in my chest when familiar steel-gray eyes met mine.

CHaPTer
Fourteen

THERE is this saying I heard once, something about being careful what you wish for, it may just come true. Yeah, that saying popped into my head as I scooted down off the bar and stood face to face with Lance. My next thought was, *I wonder if tequila can be absorbed through the skin?* I'd had a shitload of the stuff poured into and sucked out of my navel, shot glasses without a proper seal dribbled down my chest, shoulders, and arms. I was convinced it could be, and obviously once it was absorbed, it went straight to your brain and fucked with you. Because I was sure Lance would *not* be in a gay club, and he sure as hell wouldn't have been kissing a dude in public.

I reached out and poked his chest. Yup, he was real. "Are you lost?"

"No."

For some reason I couldn't identify, I felt uncomfortable standing there exposed. I snapped up my shirt and tucked it in, much to the disappointment of my new adoring fans. "Aww, c'mon, I was next!" one called out; another started chanting, "Take it off."

I shook my head at their antics, turned around, and bowed dramatically. "Sorry, this tequila boy needs a break."

"Hurry back."

I didn't make any promises. I winked and turned back to face Lance. I cocked my head and studied him. His expression was smug, confident even, as evidenced by the wide, shit-eating grin, like he knew I was choosing him over them. I was about to wipe it off. "You see those women over there?" I indicated behind me with a jerk of my head.

Lance's eyes settled on the group behind me sitting at a table, then back to mine. "Yeah, what about them?"

"Those aren't real women," I said. I leaned in a little closer and in a stage whisper, added, "They're in drag."

Lance's brows creased. "I already figured that out, Danny. What's your point?"

"My point is, there aren't any real"—I made the universal gesture for quotation marks with my fingers—"women in this club. It's a gay bar, where gay men get together to meet, drink, dance, and anything else they may take a notion to do. Naughty things. Together."

I don't know if he was waiting for the punch line to a joke or what, but Lance didn't say a word, just continued to stare at me with that befuddled expression.

I sighed. "What are you doing here and how much have you had to drink?"

"Long enough to know I'm not leaving without you and not a drop. Think of me as your designated driver."

"I don't need one." I needed to get frickin' laid, dammit! As deliriously happy as I was that Lance was there, that he'd actually shown up and given the birthday boy a kiss, it didn't change anything.

I started to walk away, but he grabbed my arm, halting my movements. I stumbled at the sudden stop and he caught me in his arms. "I think you do."

"I didn't plan on driving myself home."

Lance's face fell and he looked as if I'd punched him in the gut. After a tense moment of silence, where I wasn't sure if he was going to bolt or throw me over his shoulder and manhandle me out of the club, his shoulders slumped and I saw, rather than heard, him sigh.

"I know why you're here and it's killing me." He reached up and gently stroked my cheek with the back of his hand. "I want to be the one to spend your birthday with you."

Lance wasn't the only one in the Scarlet Romeo who felt like they were dying. I had missed him, and although I had tried my best not to think of him, I was powerless against the feelings I had for him. I knew on some level, even as I stood there mentally battling with myself between what I should do and what I wanted, that I would give in to him.

He moved his hand from my face to my waist and said, "Come dance with me?"

Although the decision had been made—I mean really, there was no choice, at least not where my heart was concerned—I still hesitated. My mouth was dry and heart pounding so hard I thought for sure he could see it beating through my chest. As the adrenaline pumped through my veins, the fight-or-flight response in full overload, I was frozen as the last of my logical side tried one last time to make my heart see reason.

"Just one dance. Please, Danny, just one," he pleaded.

My heart roared triumphantly, beating even faster as I allowed Lance to lead me to the dance floor. My mind was weeping with what it knew was to come later; it was silenced when Lance pulled me to him and began to move to the slow, sensual rhythm that filled the club, my treacherous body melting into his.

His hands roamed along my back, almost reverently, like he was memorizing, or perhaps reacquainting himself with my form. He didn't say anything, his head nestled against mine, and I could feel his breath, his lips as they brushed against my hair. However, I needed to understand. I hated being confused.

I pulled back so I could meet his eyes. "I don't understand you."

"It's okay. I don't understand me either."

"Please just tell me what it is you want from me, because I gotta tell you, I'm lost here."

"I know you planned to never see me again. I get that. Hell, I don't blame you. I wouldn't want to see me again either, after the way I've been treating you, but...." He tipped his head back and stared upward for a moment.

Was he praying? I didn't know enough about him to even guess if he believed in a higher being and yet, for someone I barely knew beyond the flesh, he had more power over me than any person I'd ever known.

When he looked at me once again, his smile was sad. "One last memory before you go?"

It wasn't a statement, he was asking, and in that moment, I was prepared to give him anything.

What a fool I was.

"YOUR friends looked disappointed you were leaving, especially that big guy," Lance said as we pulled away from the club.

Against my better judgment, I had agreed to spend the night with him. One last time he had said, and like the glutton for punishment I was, I had allowed him to lead me out of the club and usher me into his car.

"Yeah. Let's just hope Drake isn't the only one disappointed tonight." I slumped in the seat.

"C'mon, Danny. You're supposed to be having fun on your birthday. I'm going to do my damndest not to disappoint." He gave me a sidelong glance. His smile looked way happier than I felt at that moment. "I got you a present and everything."

Christ, I was such a drama queen. He was right, of course. I'd made my choice and it was stupid not to enjoy it. Live in the moment, have as much fun as possible, and worry about the consequences in the morning. That attitude had worked for me in the past.

"Yeah? What is it?"

"You're just going to have to wait and see."

"And exactly where are we going and how long is it going to take before I get my gift?"

"Not long at all," he chuckled. "We're here." Lance pulled into a hotel parking lot, drove around to the back and pulled into a space close to the entrance.

"You're renting us a room?"

"Already did. Come on," he said and stepped out of the car.

I scrambled to get out. "You did what?"

Lance stopped at the front of the car and held out his hand. "I already rented us a room."

I took his hand and, much to my chagrin, he entwined our fingers, and we walked hand in hand to the door. He pulled a key card from his back pocket and slid it into the reader. It turned green, and I heard the distinct sound of the lock disengaging. Holy hell, he really had gotten us a room.

"You really are a confident and cocky son of a bitch, aren't you?"

He shrugged. "Sometimes."

I followed him down the hall to room 1029 and again he used his key card.

"So what was Plan B if I'd refused?"

"Just like my career choice, there is no Plan B." He held the door open for me. "I'd have used brute and brawn to get my way." He winked, but I had a feeling he just might have gone all caveman had it been necessary and I might just have enjoyed it. A little.

He hadn't been kidding when he said there was no backup plan. The room itself wasn't anything special. The typical generic landscape pictures on the wall, ugly brown and burgundy quilted bedspread on the king-size bed, small TV, desk, lamp, the same you could find in thousands of hotel rooms across the country. It was what Lance had added to the room that made it exclusively for me.

White pillows from the bed had been set on the floor in the middle of the room, surrounded by balloons of purple, pink, and white held down by streamers of ribbon to metallic silver-wrapped boxes. A matching silver bucket cradled a bottle of champagne and two glass flutes sat next to it.

I walked farther into the room, tapping at a balloon and making it bob. I felt giddy, a huge smile on my face at the lengths he'd gone to for me. There was even more to him than I ever realized. Beneath the brawn wasn't only a witty and caring man, but also one hell of a romantic soul.

A large vase of wildflowers and ferns sat on the bedside table with a small white card that read "Danny." It was corny, a cliché, unoriginal, and I'd seen the same setup in numerous low-budget sappy films, but for me, it was the most romantic thing I'd ever seen. "You did all this for me?" I asked. My voice cracked with emotion as I ran a finger over the delicate petals of a purple bud.

"I wanted to make it special."

"I don't understand you." I repeated my sentiment from earlier, and I truly didn't.

Lance's warm body pressed up against my back, his strong arms encircled my waist. "Then don't try."

A slow fire burn began in my belly as Lance turned me around and kissed me tenderly. It was soft and gentle, the kind meant to soothe and explore, not excite. Yet, as Lance sucked languidly on my lower lip, nipping and licking at it, the heat increased. The warmth spread out through my body. My face felt flushed, and I hardened in response.

"You keep doing that and I won't be able to think."

"Then I'll keep doing it." His breath was hot and smelled like warm cinnamon from the gum he'd been chewing.

I wanted him to devour me. Wanted him to turn all that raw power loose. I knew he was holding back. Could feel it just below the surface in his shaking muscles, simmering and waiting to burst forth. I couldn't vocalize my need, my tongue felt too thick in my mouth. I pressed closer, body vibrating and begging for more.

Lance gave a grunt in the back of his throat, as if he were responding to my plea. He fisted his hands in my hair, tilting my head to the side, and smashed our mouths together. I got a glimpse of what he had to offer in the form of teeth clacking together as he hungrily ate at my mouth, the hot, wet kiss going on and on until my knees went weak and the only thing keeping me upright was Lance's strength.

The entire night had been a roller-coaster ride of sexual tension. The smells and sights of the club, the press of strangers, Drake's body against mine as we danced, and the body shots had kept me in a perpetual state of arousal all evening. But it was nothing compared to the feel of Lance's cock pressed against my granite-hard rod, rubbing, rubbing, rubbing, the heat and friction so good. I could have come just from that, but I wanted more. My hands itched to touch him, to feel his hot, smooth skin. I wanted him naked.

I fumbled with his T-shirt, tugging and pulling until it came free from the waistband of his jeans. My hands instantly went to his hard chest, the lightly furred flesh sweaty and damp beneath my fingers. I rubbed my thumb over one small nub, flicking it back and forth till it was hard, then pinched it lightly, pulling a deep rumbling moan from

Lance I felt vibrate on my tongue. I know I have described the sound that comes out of Lance as a deep rumble before, but it is the only description I can think of to use. It's like the purr of a giant cat: it starts low in his belly and moves upward, the sound growing in strength. It's not only audible but physical. You can feel it... well, rumbling much as the ground vibrates during a loud explosion, not necessarily in volume but definitely in intensity. It's not a roar when it escapes his lips, but a toe-curling sound that is full of passion and makes me weak. I've come to associate the sound with Lance and what I can do to him. It's oh-so-very sexy.

I gave the other nipple the same treatment until it, too, was erect. I jerked back from the kiss, grabbed the soft cotton of his shirt, shoved it upward with both hands, and sucked his right nipple into my mouth. I hummed as I sucked, teased, and tasted the salty flavor of his skin.

Lance groaned, his back arching, and the hand in my hair tightened, no longer pulling and tugging but pressing my mouth harder against him. Lance cried out when I scraped my teeth over the hard nub and bit down slightly. I started to kiss my way down his body, the soft hairs ticklish against my lips, one hand releasing his shirt and going to the button of his jeans.

"Wait." Lance stopped my movements, pressing his hand over mine.

I looked up to see his chest rising and falling rapidly as he panted for breath. I tried to pull my hand free, but he refused to let me go. I had the distinct feeling he was trying to get his arousal under control, the grip in my hair once again tugging, keeping my mouth away from his skin.

After a few more deep breaths, he began to chuckle. "Damn, that was close."

"I thought that was the goal?" I pushed out my bottom lip and pouted.

"Presents first."

I arched a brow at him. "I was trying to unwrap my gift and you stopped me."

I was still pouting when he laughed, pulled me upright and kissed my protruding bottom lip. "God, that's a powerful tool."

"So I get my way?"

I reached for his button again but he lightly slapped my hand away. "Yes, but the other presents first."

"Not powerful enough," I grumbled under my breath.

Lance heard it and only laughed harder, and then pushed me back until I was sitting on the edge of the bed. "You can be such a spoiled brat, you do know that, right?" he asked and handed me a brightly colored wrapped box he'd retrieved from the dresser.

"One of my best attributes," I teased and accepted the gift. It was heavy and I shook it, but nothing rattled around.

"Definitely a brat." Lance sat next to me and bumped me with his shoulder. "Just open it."

I tore the paper away; it was a gift box of oils, lotions, and powder. Nice, but not as nice as the package I was really craving. "Thanks."

"It's not what you think, honest. I got it in the men's department," he said quickly, his cheeks turning pink. "And it's only part of the gift. Take your clothes off and lie on the bed." He took the box and stood.

I ripped open my shirt. "Now you're talking!"

CHaPTer
FIFTeen

LANCE removed the bottle of oil from the box, snapped the top open, pouring a generous amount into his palm. His eyes heavy on me as I dropped my shirt and pulled the belt free from my jeans made my skin tingle with excitement. He rubbed his big hands together, warming the oil. I couldn't wait to feel them against my flesh and quickly shoved my jeans down, stepping out of them and kicking them away.

I hesitated, thumbs hooked in the waistband of the black boy shorts. I was hard, my erection bulging beneath the cotton material, but held against my body. Suddenly I felt unsure. Would removing them strip away the last of the fantasy? I had never been completely naked in front of Lance. Would seeing me completely bare and on display for him turn him off? Would it be too much for him to handle?

Lance stepped closer, brushed his lips against mine, and as if he had been reading my thoughts, said, "I promise you, Danny, *all* of you is part of my fantasy."

I sucked in a breath, held it, shoved the shorts down, and added them to the pile of my other discarded clothes. Lance took a step back and it was as if time stood still, while his eyes wandered down my body.

"You're so beautiful," he murmured. "I want to touch you, all of you."

I let out the breath and tried not to hyperventilate, his words sending my pulse soaring. It felt like my heart was trying to pound its way out of my chest. On shaky legs, I crawled into the middle of the bed and lay on my stomach, the soft cotton cool against my heated flesh. I was still feeling too vulnerable and unsure to lie fully exposed.

Lance climbed on top of me, straddling my butt. I jerked when his slick hands touched my shoulders, and then moaned as he began to knead the tense muscles there. The room was silent, other than the sounds of our shared breaths, as Lance massaged and caressed every inch of my back. His palms pressed hard against my lower back and ran up each side of my spine.

It felt so good and I moaned my pleasure.

He chuckled at my response and skimmed his fingers down each bony protrusion of my spine. It tickled and I squirmed beneath him.

His hands moved to my waist, barely skimming across the area. "Are you ticklish?"

"Lance," I warned through gritted teeth. I lifted my head from where it rested on my folded arm and glared back at him.

He removed his hands and held them up in a defensive manner. "Just checking."

He then scooted back, sitting on my thighs, and dug his fingers into the globes of my ass, my dick twitched against my stomach in response. His thumbs rubbed and teased up and down along my crease until I thought I would go out of my mind, and then they were gone. Both his strong hands massaged down my right leg to my foot, then back up my left. I was hard and horny, yet his ministrations were melting me right into the soft mattress below.

"Roll over so I can do the front."

I did as he asked. The rough inside seam of Lance's jeans felt abrasive against my legs as I rolled beneath him. My head cradled in the downy softness of the pillow, I rested my arms above me. Without taking his gaze from my body, Lance leaned over and grabbed the oil from where he'd set it on the bedside table and poured more into his palm. He rubbed his hands together again, warming the oil, and started at my knees.

I couldn't take my eyes from him. His expression was one of awe and wonderment as he explored my body, finding all the small areas that made me twitch and squirm. The inside of my thighs, my hips, below my armpits, but never where I wanted to feel his touch the most. "Please" was on the tip of my tongue. I wanted to beg him to wrap those wonderfully talented hands around my cock and relieve the ache.

But he was so sexy, his gray eyes constantly moving over me, nibbling his bottom lip in concentration.

"So soft, yet so strong," he said absently as he traced the ridges of my chest.

Normally I was the aggressor—not that Lance couldn't be aggressive, he could, but I always had to push him to it. This new side of him thrilled me, as much as being naked and vulnerable while he was fully clothed did. He was making this completely about me and I found it hot as fuck. My cock agreed, straining, curving upward toward my stomach.

I fisted the pillow to keep from reaching out to touch him and clenched my jaw to keep from begging for more. I didn't want to break the spell Lance seemed to be under, but I didn't know how much more I could take.

I was pushed even closer to the verge of insanity when Lance leaned in further as he worked his way up my arms, his breath warm against my mouth. "I never appreciated how truly sexy you are."

"I'm even sexier with a naked body rubbing all over me."

"Oh really?" Lance chuckled then pushed his tongue into my mouth, and I could only nod, hoping like hell he believed me.

Oh and thank you, Jesus, Mary, and Joseph, and anyone who may have had a hand in answering my prayer when Lance left me breathless as the kiss ended and then leaned back and whipped off his shirt, throwing it to the side.

His muscles bulged and sweat glistened on his golden skin. He was too much of a temptation and I propped myself up on my elbows and licked the salty dampness.

Lance gasped then shoved me back. "Ah, ah, ah." He twitched a finger at me—I was tempted to bite it. "I'm not done giving you your gift yet."

I dropped back onto the pillow and grunted.

"You seem a little tense. Aren't you enjoying your relaxing massage?"

I looked down my body to my oozing, neglected cock. The head swollen, dark and ruddy it was so engorged. I was so hard it hurt. When I looked back up at him, his eyes were twinkling—fucking twinkling—

and his smile was sly. He was enjoying this way too much. Okay, I admit, so was I, but I was beginning to think I was at the point where shit exploding was becoming a very real danger.

I snaked a hand out and grabbed his left nipple, pinching it. Hard.

"Ow!" He swatted my hand away. "Okay, I get it. Moving along now."

I watched, transfixed, as Lance leaned in and ran the tip of his tongue down my chest, scooting toward the end of the bed as he left a wet trail down to my navel. I sucked in a harsh breath when he dipped inside the small indent. I shuddered when he nuzzled my cock, the stubble on his jaw harsh against the delicate skin.

"That feels so good," I murmured.

Lance fisted my cock, squeezing it until the veins stood out, and pressed it harder against his cheek, scraping, scratching. It was almost too much, but it felt so fucking good, the little flare of pain adding to the pleasure. Even better was that it was Lance doing it. He'd jerked me off, rubbed his cock against mine, but had never had it this close to his mouth.

Without warning, Lance sucked me into his mouth, making wet slurping noises as he bobbed his head up and down. He didn't take much, only a couple of inches before pulling back again, but he'd made a tight seal with his lips and each pass stuttered over the ridge of my cock head.

Oh fuck! I thought. *I'm going to come!* I'd been dreaming of Lance's mouth on my dick, wanted it, and I was going to blow before I could fully enjoy it.

"Wait! Shit! Wait!"

Lance lifted his head, eyes wild and a little glazed. "What? Did I do something wrong?"

"Uh, no." A snort of laughter escaped me through panting breaths and I shook my head. "Too right."

Lance's smile was smug. "I had a good teacher." Then he was sucking me back into his mouth.

My eyes nearly rolled back in my head, lids heavy and threatening to close, but I forced them to stay open. I didn't want to miss a second of this. Lance nursed at my dick, teeth threatening and sending shivers up my spine. It wasn't the best blowjob I'd ever had—he couldn't take me in very far without gagging—but what he lacked in experience, he more than made up for in enthusiasm. Watching him, head bobbing, cheeks hollowing as he sucked hard, drool running down from the corners of his mouth, was the hottest thing I'd ever seen. Straight boy Lance Lenard was sucking my dick and when he looked up at me through long curling lashes, there was so much lust in his eyes I knew he was loving it too. That look alone had me gripping the sheet in my fists, tensing and fighting to hold back my orgasm.

Then cool air hit my wet dick when Lance surged up, sitting back on his heels, pumping his cock hard. When the hell had he lost his pants? I only contemplated it for a moment, though, because really, I didn't fucking care when he had. His big hand pumped his thick shaft, the veins standing out, head lolled back, and he snapped his hips and shouted.

I felt the hot liquid land on my cock, stomach, and even in the hollow of my throat, but I couldn't look away from his gorgeous face. Mouth open wide, his shout turning to a silent scream. I had thought seeing Lance gobbling down my cock was the hottest thing I'd ever seen, but I was wrong. Watching him, skin flushed, damp with sweat, wild as he jerked and danced with abandoned pleasure above me, was the most magnificent thing I'd ever seen.

"Christ, sorry about that." His smile was timid, cheeks darkening further.

He had nothing to be sorry for, nothing at all. And then. *Oh. My. God.* He scooped up his spunk from my chest and brought his hand to his mouth, licking and sucking the cream from his fingers. I knew I had to be dreaming. I knew I was going to wake up in the morning with a hell of a hangover and sticky sheets because no way was this real.

When Lance started sucking my shaft again, I grabbed his head in both my hands, started fucking his face hard, and he took it. Nostrils flaring, face turning red, but he hummed as if he wanted more. It was my dream, so of course he wanted more—and I gave it to him.

"That's it. Take it all."

I thrust hard as I pulled his head down, and this time my eyes did roll back in my skull when I felt the flared head push into his throat, the muscles contracting around it, and my thin grasp on control was shredded and stripped away. I came so hard I saw stars dance behind my closed lids.

The sound of coughing and sputtering brought me back down from the high. I opened my eyes to find Lance wiping at his mouth, eyes watering as he fought to catch his breath.

Nearly choking Lance to death wasn't part of the fantasy. "Jesus!" I scrambled to sit up, banging my head against the headboard. That felt way too fucking real to be a dream. "I'm so sorry, Lance. I got a little—"

Lance licked his wet lips and waggled his brow at me. "Guess we're even now, huh? I'm fine. You just caught me off guard is all."

I bet not as much as I was when he sat atop my thighs and kissed me, feeding me my own flavor. Lance was thorough in his exploration of my mouth, humming and sounding so damn content and happy, like he was thanking me. Like he wasn't the one who had just given me the best birthday gift I'd ever received.

Regret swam through the desire, turning into a raw pain that twisted my heart as I sat there kissing him. The effect of his body against mine, the warm, wet tongue so gentle and yet dominant, wasn't the only thing that stole my breath. I had fallen hard for him, I knew that in the center of my very being, and yet tomorrow it would be over. Lance would go back to his jock boy ways, sweet little blonde girl on his arm as he moved a step closer to his dream.

Me?

I stared into those amazing gray eyes that had haunted me since the first moment I'd seen them and knew. Tomorrow I'd be doing my best to glue back the pieces of my broken heart.

CHAPTER
SIXTEEN

THE sun pouring in through the partially open curtains burned at my red and raw eyes. I squinted at the clock on the bedside table and groaned. It was just after eleven, only four hours since Lance and I had finally given up on the record for most orgasms in one night and collapsed together in a tangle of arms and limbs.

I buried my face into his side and pulled the covers up over my head. I needed more sleep. Maybe with another hour or two the slight throb in my brain would be gone. I knew it would do nothing for the soreness in my muscles or the ache in my nut sac though—I'd be feeling those effects for days.

Somewhere outside the window, a car horn blared and a door slammed in the hallway. Life was going on around me, but I was buried in my cocoon, surrounded by the smell of sex, sweat, and Lance, and my mind wandered back to the night before—or rather, earlier in the morning.

When I had left my dorm the day before, I had one goal in mind, to fuck or be fucked. Yes, I know, shallow, maybe even a little slutty, but I was twenty-one, single, and horny. I make no excuses for my behavior. I had no idea what I'd actually get was much better than my simple carnal wish.

I got sexy in the form of a full-body massage culminating in a sloppy blowjob and a sixty-nine. Better yet, I experienced raw, visceral, and dirty fun. And, although I would have sworn four short hours ago that I'd never be able to get it up again, the images of him on his knees in the shower, licking droplets of water off my skin, had my cock swelling until it poked against Lance's lightly furred thigh.

It wasn't just the hot coupling that made it the best celebration ever—it was Lance himself that had been the best part, the real surprise gift. The room he'd set up with balloons, flowers, and champagne gave me a glimpse of his cheesy romantic side. The way he touched me, stroking my face as he kissed me or the way he cradled me in his arms while we came down from an orgasm, showed me his tender side. His laughter as I painted his chest with champagne and the look in his eyes when I licked it off were images and memories that would forever be seared into my brain. Ones that would torment and haunt, scabs to be picked at so they never healed.

With that sorrowful thought, I knew I would never get back to sleep—the pain in my head, and the deeper one in my chest, would not allow it. I placed a kiss to Lance's chest and, careful not to wake him, slipped quietly from the bed. I gathered my discarded clothes and dressed. My movements felt sluggish from a weariness that had nothing to do with exhaustion. After I slipped into my boots, I stood at the side of the bed and watched Lance sleep.

Another image that would forever be with me. He looked so at ease, his broad chest rising and falling in a slow, even rhythm. His face slack in slumber, even more handsome than usual. I kissed the tip of my index finger and softly brushed it over his parted lips. I jerked my hand back when he stirred and held my breath. His brows creased slightly, but he never opened his eyes. Had he known I was there placing one last kiss to his lips? Did he know I was leaving?

Tears blurred my vision, threatening to spill. I would not cry. He had to have known what was coming, known last night it was our last time. Perhaps I was doing it the cowardly way—fine, I was a coward—but I couldn't say it. I'd been on such an emotional rollercoaster since seeing Lance with the little blonde thing. It really was at that moment when I'd realized I had to end it, if for no other reason than my own sanity. I was the one who took it past casual sex and experimentation, and I also knew that walking away without saying good-bye was a really shitty thing to do to Lance. As I stood there watching him sleep, I knew what I was about to do was wrong. He didn't deserve it, yet at the time, I was already trying to distance myself and push him back into that box labeled "casual sex partner." The first step toward that was to avoid the awkward morning after, as I had done so many times in the past.

I grabbed the gift box from the floor and hurried out the door, closing it silently behind me.

THROUGH the cab ride back to my car and the drive back to campus, I replayed every minute of the night before. From the moment the blindfold was pulled from my eyes and I found Lance standing over me, to the moment I walked out the door of the hotel room and left him sleeping. I plowed through a barrage of emotions from elation to despair and by the time I walked through the door of my dorm, I was physically exhausted and emotionally sick.

Thank God Bo wasn't there. I shucked out of my clothes and crawled beneath the covers. The sheets were cold, nothing like the warmth of the bed I'd shared with Lance, and I shuddered. I was too tired to think anymore, I'd gone numb, and it took no time at all before I fell into a fitful sleep.

It was hours later when I was shaken awake. "Danny. Dude, where the hell have you been?" Bo's voice sounded upset and I pulled the covers off my head and rubbed my eyes against the harsh light so I could glare at Bo without my retinas catching fire.

"What do you mean where the hell I've been? I'm obviously sleeping, asshole," I grumbled, pulled the covers back up over my head, and turned my back to him.

Bo ripped the covers from my head. "Hey!"

"You had everyone scared shitless, you fucker! Lance called, panicking, said you had gone missing and weren't answering your phone." Bo waved his hands wildly, spittle flying out of his mouth as he continued to rant. "What the hell is, like, wrong with you? We've been trying to get ahold of you for, like, two hours!"

"What are you, like a valley girl now?" I grabbed my covers and pulled them back up, but I didn't cover my head this time. "Well, you're not the smartest chick if it took you two hours to check the one place I would most likely be. Now, do you mind? I'm going back to sleep."

"No, you're not. You're going to call Lance and tell him you're okay."

The fuck I was. "This doesn't concern you."

"Really? Because I'm thinking that my best friend—with whom I thought we shared everything—has been lying to me for months does concern me."

I scrubbed a hand across my face and sighed. "I couldn't tell you."

Bo shoved my legs up and out of the way and sat across the end of the bed, leaning back against the wall. "He showed up at Katie's place needing to talk to her alone. He looks bad, Danny. What happened?"

My stomach rolled as shame assaulted me. I could have left him a note, woken him and told him I was leaving. I shook those thoughts away. I had done the right thing by leaving, and it wouldn't have made a damn bit of difference how I did it—the outcome would be the same. Would it have made any difference if he'd seen how hard it was for me? Would letting him see the tears that poured from my eyes when I walked down that hallway make this any easier for him? Wasn't it better that I let him think I was a prick and had just cast him aside when I was done with him?

"Danny?"

I scooted around on the bed until I was sitting next to him and leaned my head on his shoulder. "Where should I start?" I whispered and took his hand in mine.

He squeezed my hand. "From the beginning, I guess."

So I did.

I told him about the stripper and Lance's attraction to me. I didn't go into graphic detail, but I shared with him how it started out as an ego boost and a fantasy for me, an experiment on Lance's part. The early morning texts, the tenderness and real friendship that started to grow, the moments when I began to realize that I wanted the impossible, when I began to fall for him. Through it all, Bo just held my hand and let me pour my soul out to him without saying a word.

When I recounted our trip earlier in the week and how I felt when I saw Lance kissing that girl, and what I did afterward, Bo finally interrupted me.

"If it makes you feel better, he wasn't cheating on her with you."

"How do you know that?" I asked.

"I mean, I think he was when you two first got together, but he ended things with Morgan months ago."

So the girlfriend had a name. I'd always wondered, but it probably wouldn't have mattered—I'd have still referred to her as the blonde bimbo. "He left his cell phone at her house. I saw them together. Trust me, he's still with her."

Bo shook his head. "Morgan and Katie are good friends. I didn't hear what Morgan had to say, but I heard Katie's response the thousand times Morgan called. Jesus, that chick talks a lot."

"You picked her."

"Not Katie, you ass, Morgan." I lifted my brows at him and he laughed. "Okay, she talks a lot too, but Morgan's got her beat."

"Wow!"

"I know," he said, still laughing. "Anyway, Morgan wanted Katie to talk to Lance. Try and talk him into going back to her, but from what Katie said, Lance kept saying he couldn't. He wouldn't tell Katie or Morgan why, only that it wouldn't be fair. When Katie finally cornered him and forced him to tell her what was going on and what he meant by it not being fair, he said he needed to focus more on football and his studies. That he cared about Morgan but wasn't in love with her. That was all he would say, but Katie was sure there was more to it."

"Bo, I'm telling you, I saw them together."

"I don't know what you saw, but he ain't with her."

"What about the cell phone he left at her house?" I asked skeptically.

"From what I heard, Lance was hanging out with some of his old friends and Morgan found out and showed up. Lance left when she caused a scene, but he either dropped his cell phone or, more than likely, she swiped it."

Okay, my behavior after seeing the two of them together just added to the pile of guilt and feeling of douchebaggery. I probably owed Lance an apology, but even as I thought it, I knew it wouldn't happen. It changed nothing in the grand scheme of things. I think Lance knew it too. It explained why he didn't tell me he'd broken things off with her and let me believe they were a couple. He couldn't ever have a relationship with me and I simply couldn't continue to see him, certainly couldn't touch him, and hide my true feelings for him anymore.

When I didn't say anything, Bo finally asked, "Are you going to talk to him?"

"I don't think so."

"Can I ask why? He's obviously crazy about you."

"He'll be three years out of high school during the next draft."

"And?" he asked, confused.

"Yeah, I had the same reaction. Lance's dream is to play in the NFL."

Bo looked at me with a confused expression on his face.

"It's the one thing he wants most and will do anything to achieve his goal. He doesn't have a Plan B."

After a moment, Bo frowned and looked down at our hands. "And if people found out about the two of you—"

"No dream," I finished for him.

"That sucks," he said sincerely and pulled his hand from mine to wrap an arm around me.

I snuggled in closer and nodded. "Yup."

"Any chance you can still be friends?"

"No. Mike's already been starting rumors about Lance coming over here. Lance didn't say it, but I'm pretty sure that's why he stopped coming over and started having me meet him instead of picking me up." My chest felt heavy, like someone was standing on it, stealing my breath when I thought about having to be in the same room with Lance and not be able to touch him. "I mean, I can be friendly toward him when I'm with you and Katie, but I don't see that happening a lot anymore." I swallowed hard, trying to dislodge the lump that had formed in my throat. My voice still cracked with the swell of emotion when I admitted, "And to be honest, I think it would be too hard for us. I know it would for me. At least for a while."

"Worse than Cody?"

"That wasn't love—that was teenage hormones gone wild."

"And now you know the difference?"

I could only nod and try not to puke, or cry, or suffocate. All three were possible and it sucked.

"No offense, but Jesus, I'm glad I'm not gay. I have enough trouble with relationships without all the added bullshit you have to deal with."

"Yeah, it can be rough sometimes, but the sex is way better."

"Like you would know."

I sat up and glared at him. "Stephanie Croft?"

Bo rolled his eyes at me. "You only made it to second base, that doesn't count."

I gave him a saucy smile. "Yeah, but I hit a home run with her brother."

"All-state baseball and basketball star David Croft, notorious skirt chaser, so did not do you." He popped me in the arm and then scurried off the bed before I could hit him back. "In your dreams, Marshal."

"Oh, please! He's a big ol' queen. Last I heard he was living with his boyfriend down in Toledo. Besides, I never said he did me." I gave him a naughty look.

Bo's mouth fell open and he gaped at me when it dawned on him who was bending over. "Jesus!"

I just grinned.

"C'mon, get dressed. We'll go get a gallon of double-fudge ice cream and rent a couple of sappy chick flicks. I'll let you snot on my sleeve and you'll feel better in the morning."

"Aww, just like I did for you when Amy Minz broke your heart."

"Whatever. You rented Predator and gave me a box of Milk Duds."

"And you bawled like a baby," I teased, slipping on a sweatshirt and jeans.

"My allergies were acting up!"

"Mmm hmm," I murmured as I pulled on my tennis shoes.

"They were!" he said sharply, but he was smiling when he held the door open for me.

I stopped and went up on my tiptoes and kissed his cheek. "Thanks," I said sincerely.

"Anytime."

I doubted I'd feel a whole lot better by morning, but spending the evening snuggled up with my best friend, with double-chocolate ice cream, sure beat the hell out of staring at the ceiling all alone.

CAN we talk?

I stared down at the text and just like the day before, and the day before that, I ignored it. I still wasn't sure what I wanted to say to him, if anything. I dropped the phone back onto the bed and covered my head with the blanket.

I should have been in class, doing something, anything to get my mind off Lance. The whole past week—hell, the previous month—had been totally craptastic. I'd made the decision to stop seeing Lance the day we'd gone to pick up his phone. Yeah, I felt guilty as hell for not giving him any explanation, but, Jesus, after what I told him on the way back from the Unity, I'm sure he knew why. *"There is no Plan B."* I was convinced he would have been perfectly happy with the whole *let's fuck when we can and pretend we're nothing more than friends when we're in public,* but I couldn't. For me, Lance had become more than just a friend—or rather, I wanted us to be.

It wasn't until right before I was to leave for New York, numerous pleas from Katie, and a little time away from him to come to terms with my feelings for Lance, that I finally gave in and agreed to talk to him.

He'd sent one of his now familiar *Can we talk?* texts, and after taking a deep breath, I hit the Call button.

"Danny?"

"Yeah, it's me," I said, my heart in my throat.

There was a long pause on the other end, and suddenly I wasn't sure why I had called him, or that I wanted to hear what I knew he would say. I leaned back against the headboard and pulled my knees up, hugging them.

"I want to talk to you. Can I come over?"

I blew out a ragged breath. "I don't think that's such a good idea."

"Come on, Danny, just for a few minutes." His voice was pleading.

The tone of his voice had me nearly giving in and agreeing, but thankfully the more rational part of my brain told my heart to back the fuck up, and took over. "Then talk. I'm listening."

He was quiet for a second. Then he said in a low voice, "I just want to see you. Please, I've missed you."

"Don't say shit like that," I told him with a sigh as I rubbed at my burning eyes.

"Well I have," he insisted.

"Is it me you miss or your experimentation?"

"You."

"Bullshit," I bit out, my anger instantly flaring. I'd been a fool to think I had come to terms with my feelings for Lance. As unfair as it might have been, I lashed out as all the conflicting emotions came rushing to the surface. "You barely fucking know me beyond the bedroom."

"I know plenty about you, and if you give me the chance, I want to learn a lot more." His voice sounded sincere, which for some reason only infuriated me more.

I wanted to know everything about him, and in turn, I wanted him to know everything about me, and therein was the problem. Had I been able to keep my feelings for him on a friendship basis, none of this would have been an issue. But no matter how hard I tried to convince my heart that Lance was not, nor would he ever be, able to love it back, the damn thing hadn't listened.

"So you want to come over, do you? Because you miss me?"

"Yeah."

My defense mechanism for hiding my hurt, Mr. Happy-go-lucky, was firmly in place when I said, "Okay, sure, come on over. I'm sure I can convince Mike, my nosey neighbor, who is a total rumor whore and has become very interested in your comings and goings from my room, that you and I are just a couple of buds hanging out to chat."

I heard his barely audible curse of *shit*, but he didn't say anything more.

I figured I'd help him out. "Oh wait!" I snapped my fingers close to the phone. "You probably already heard the rumors since you suddenly stopped coming over. Maybe you should just pick me up. How far down the block would you like me to walk so no one sees the fag getting in the car?"

"Danny—"

"I can call Bo and Katie and ask them to join us at the coffee shop." I was getting more and more pissed off as I spoke, and it took a real effort to keep the bitterness out of my voice.

"Jesus. Why are you so pissed off? I'm not the one who left you in a fucking motel room without so much as a good-bye, but suddenly I'm the bad guy here?"

The anger in Lance's voice shredded my tentative hold on my own infuriation. "No, you're the guy who wants me to suck his dick in private but can't be seen with said cocksucker in public."

"That's not fair. You know how important it is for me to make the NFL. Do you have any idea what my teammates would do if they found out I was messing with a dude?" Lance asked in a strained, incredulous voice.

"I can only imagine how disgusted they would be," I said in a barely controlled voice. "I'm going to do you a favor and help you with that little problem."

I hit the End button and threw the phone across the room. "Son of a bitch!" I screamed angrily. I got up from the bed and paced the small area of my dorm. Lance hadn't told me anything I hadn't already known. The irritating ache in my chest was proof that at least one part of me had been hoping I was wrong. The tears that dampened my cheeks as I continued to stomp and rage attested to just how heartbroken I was.

cHapTer
sevenTeen

Three years later

WHEN it felt like the world was closing in on me, the hustle and bustle of New York City was making my head pound, and I needed to escape the noise and crowded streets, my small studio apartment was like a sanctuary. For some I suppose it would seem a bit crowded, overstimulating, and not calm in the slightest. However, for me, the vibrant colors, the mishmash of collectables, and the cluttered walls, full of posters, theater masks, photos, and feather boas were comforting. I'd transplanted my dorm room to this place, added to it each week, combined the past and present. It was a constant reminder of where I came from, where I was, and where I was going.

Nestled in its folds, the place held both happiness and sorrow. Perhaps that was what put me at ease—balance.

Standing at the window, staring out at the New York skyline, contract in hand, I felt anything but at ease. In fact, since I'd received the document from my agent hours ago via courier, I'd felt the walls were closing in on me and found it difficult to breathe.

"It's the opportunity of a lifetime," he'd said. *"You'll be a star, baby, a huge star."* The second statement was the same one tons of model wannabes and young kids had heard when stepping into a sleazy, self-proclaimed agent to the stars' office. In my case, though, I wasn't being conned into doing porn or having to pay an exorbitant fee to some asshole who would pocket my last dime and I'd never hear from him again.

In my case, it wasn't Broadway, but my two left feet, small delicate frame, and overly theatrical movements apparently were perfect for a starring role off-Broadway. All I had to do was sign on the dotted line and I'd be whisked back to nineteenth-century London. For five two-and-a-half-hour shows each week, I'd become a womanizer, a man who made the world laugh as a legendary screen persona, but who struggled to find happiness in his own life. I would become Chaplin.

Jonathan Culvert, agent extraordinaire and good friend of my parents, was right about one thing—it was an opportunity of a lifetime. At least it was for a twenty-four-year-old young man with no experience beyond four years of university. So why was I hesitating?

I leaned my forehead against the cool window and sighed, my breath fogging up the glass, making it difficult to see, but I wasn't really looking at the view anyway.

Was it Kyle making me question signing the contract? Even as I thought it, I knew he had nothing to do with my decision, which just made me feel like a major bastard. Kyle and I had been dating for a year, and lately he'd been pressuring me to take *us* to the next level. I just didn't feel the same way about *us* as he did.

I dropped the file on the coffee table and slumped onto the couch, sprawling out and putting my hands behind my pounding head. The offer to star as Chaplin wasn't the only one on the table. I'd also been offered a part in an Olivier Award-winning drama that would be opening in Chicago. It wasn't the lead role, not as good of an opportunity as the lead role of Chaplin, but in turning it down, I was also saying no to Kyle. The only reason I'd tried out for the part was at his urging, certainly not because I'd had any real desire to move to Chicago even if he now lived there, having accepted a position with a dance troupe.

"Ugh!" I grabbed the afghan off the back of the couch, wrapped it around me, and covered my head. Twenty-four years old and I still liked to hide in my cocoons. Some things never changed.

I was hedging, but I already knew what I was going to do. I was going to take the lead role, but I hated saying good-bye to Kyle. I wasn't *in* love with him, but I did love him. We had met at a club, and it was lust at first sight for both of us. He was tall, head full of dark, nearly black, curly hair, a permanent five o'clock shadow on his jaw, and amazing midnight-blue eyes. Kyle had been dancing since he was three, and by twenty-five had the kind of body that begs to be idolized and, trust me when I tell you, I fell to my knees many, many, many times in worship.

Kyle was a great guy and we had a ton of fun when our schedules allowed us to get together. His work ethic was second to none, he was loyal, dedicated to the arts, and adored me. The sex was also hot. He could go from a soft, tender lover who wants me to make love to him all night long and cuddle for hours afterward, to a kinky and aggressive, dominant lover who can leave me walking funny for days. He kissed me and held my hand in public, comfortable with who he was, and loved to show me off as his man wherever we went. What's not to love, right? I don't know why my heart never made the leap— maybe because I knew Kyle's dream was to live in Paris, travel the world, while mine was New York, and I knew one of us would end up unhappy if we gave up our dream. Or perhaps it was as simple as my heart wasn't mine to give. I refused to dwell on the reasons behind that notion.

The ringing of my cell phone had me climbing out of my cocoon. Not because I really wanted to leave its warmth, but because I needed a distraction from where my mind was beginning to wander. That was a dangerous path with a slippery slope, one I didn't want to walk when I had so many other things on my mind that needed my focus.

I grabbed my phone from the small table by the door and smiled when I recognized Bo's number. I flipped it open. "Well if it isn't Dr. Nerd."

I loved teasing him about his career choice. I mean really, only a total geek would get his doctorate in business instead of medicine where he was sure to get laid by lots of horny, willing, gold-digging nurses.

"Katie's pregnant!" he blurted out as soon as I answered. "I don't know what the fuck I'm going to do. We're still in school, with an education debt that I'm pretty sure is right up there on the same level as the I'm-so-fucked national debt. We're not married. I can't afford to get married." His voice rose with each short choppy sentence he rambled and the panic was evident in his high-pitched tone. "Danny, what the hell am I going to do?"

"Well—"

"I'm going to suck as a dad. Drop it on its head or worse, forget it at the grocery store or park or some other obscure place. You know how I'm always forgetting where I leave shit. Remember that time I left my laptop at the library? It was my pride and joy and I just left it there unattended."

"Bo!" I yelled into the phone but if he heard me, it didn't stop him. He didn't even take a breath.

"Oh God! What if I do that to a kid? I'll scar it for life. I'll end up in jail, with a cell mate called Bubba and become his bitch, with a wife that hates me and a fucked-up kid. Danny, I'm not good with kids."

Okay, wow! I needed a distraction, but damn, I hadn't expected a nuclear meltdown.

"Danny? Danny, are you here? Did you hear me? Katie's pregnant!"

I plopped back down on the couch and couldn't help but laugh. And he called me a drama queen. "Yes I heard you. First of all, you're not going to be Bubba's bitch, you're going to be Katie's bitch for the next eighteen years."

"This isn't funny," he huffed into the phone.

"No, I suppose becoming a dad isn't a laughing matter, but your response is fucking hilarious."

"I hate you!" But I could hear the snort of laughter he was trying to hold back and could imagine him biting his lip to keep from laughing outright.

"Feel better now?"

"Yeah, I think so. I've been holding that in all night behind an 'it's going to be okay' façade to keep Katie calm. She's pretty freaked out too."

"Good. I know it's scary and might not be the best time, but you and Katie are going to be amazing parents," I said sincerely. The kid would probably be dressed in Goodwill-boring, go deaf by the age of two from Katie talking his or her ears off, but would have two amazingly loving parents.

"You really think so?"

"Yeah, Bo. I do. So when is little Bogart Humphrey, Junior making their grand entrance?"

"Katie figures she's five to six weeks, so about seven and half months, and I can assure you, I'd never be as mean to my kid as my parents were to me. Bogart won't be gracing any birth certificate except on the line 'who's your daddy'. Katie and I at least agree on that."

"Thank God," I laughed. "Talk about scarring a kid for life."

"I know, right." Bo laughed too.

"So what are you and Katie not agreeing to?"

"She wants to get married next weekend."

"You two have been together for what, four years? You've talked about getting married after graduate school and, dude, if she is willing to forego a big fancy wedding, I say go for it. Make an honest woman out of her."

"So you'll come?"

Oh shit! I walked right into that one. A trickle of unease seeped down my spine.

"You will be able to make it, won't you? I can't get married without my best friend standing up with me."

I sighed and rubbed absently at my chest. "I take it he's invited too?"

"He's her brother. We can't not invite him."

I tipped my head back on the couch and blew out a heavy breath as the unease churned in my gut. Three years I'd avoided seeing Lance Lenard and it looked like a broken condom or missed Pill or whatever was going to change that.

"I wouldn't miss it."

"Thanks. I'm not sure of all the details yet, we only just told her parents this morning and Katie and her mom have been in deep discussion ever since, but I'll let you know. Just plan on being here on the seventh so we can have one last drink before...." He laughed nervously. "Before I become a husband and soon-to-be dad."

"Geez, that sounds so weird."

"Tell me about it. Okay, I'll call you as soon as I know more."

"Sounds good. And, Bo?"

"Yeah?"

"Katie is one lucky girl. You are going to be a great husband and dad."

I ended the call and grabbed the file I'd dropped on the table, tapping it on my leg. I wasn't thrilled about seeing Lance again. Was I still in love with him? I didn't know. Hell, I wasn't really sure if I was ever *in* love with Lance or if it was the challenge, the thrill of having the ultimate impossible fantasy for a while. I didn't sit around pining and thinking of him every day. There were moments I smiled when I thought of him, others of guilt, and still at times a feeling of loss, but I never dwelled on any of those emotions. They were single moments out of hours, and I had moved on. I was chasing and achieving my dreams. The one thing I had allowed myself in three years where Lance was concerned was I had followed the NFL draft the year after I left and knew he'd been picked up by Minnesota, so I knew he had reached his dreams too.

No regrets.

I may not have been one hundred percent sure I'd been in love with Lance, but the one thing I was sure about was Kyle never made me feel the way Lance had.

I leaned over, opened the drawer on the end table, and pulled out a pen. Flipping the file open, I signed the contract and this time I didn't hesitate. That decision made, I picked my phone back up and scrolled through the contacts. Finding the number I needed, I hit Call.

"Thank you for calling Delta Airlines, how may I direct your call?" a cheery, female voice asked.

"I'd like to book a flight for Chicago."

Kyle was expecting to hear my decision, and I knew that what I was about to tell him was going to break his heart. I'd done a lot of growing up in the three years since I'd left Michigan. I was no longer a coward. I wasn't going to walk away without a word, and Kyle deserved more than a text message or a phone call.

Chapter
eighteen

THE flight from New York to Detroit was uneventful. Just like the trip I'd made the previous week, it wasn't the traveling that sucked, it was what faced me at the other end that had been the hard part.

Kyle's eyes had lit up when he'd first seen me in the hallway outside his dressing room. But he'd taken in the flowers in my hand and the expression on my face and his had fallen. He knew before I'd even opened my mouth that I'd come to tell him I wouldn't be joining him in Chicago. There had been a lot of tears, from both of us, but we also agreed that it was unfair for either of us to give up their dream. He wasn't willing to move to New York, and I wasn't willing to move to Chicago. As badly as it had sucked to say good-bye to Kyle, I was glad I had done it face-to-face, that I had chosen to do it at all and not just walk away. It gave us both closure; it still hurt, but the healing began the minute I walked out the door of his apartment and headed back to New York.

The trip to Michigan wouldn't be so easy.

I'd declined Bo's offer to stay with him and his parents, electing to rent a hotel in Pontiac not too far from Lapeer, where the wedding ceremony would take place. Bo seemed upset with my decision, but he finally relented when I explained that the club we were going to celebrate his last night of bachelordom was only two blocks away. I damn sure was going to need a drink, probably lots of drinks, since Bo had been obligated to invite Lance. Yeah, I was sure I would be in no shape to drive either of us home.

Before I left New York, I had been prepared to shave my head. I still had a dislike of wigs and I would need the new do. I sat in the chair, cringing and physically sick to my stomach as the hairdresser shaved a swatch of hair from the side of my head. The long blond locks looked obscene against the black cape. When he did the same thing to the other side, the last of the color drained from my face. I must have looked pretty bad because the guy started fanning me with a magazine and screeching,

"Honey, it's okay. Breathe! It's just hair, it will grow back."

I'd been so focused on the hair falling all around me that I hadn't even looked at my reflection in the mirror. When his screeching voice finally penetrated the fog, I looked up at my reflection and….

"Oh. My. God! I love it!"

The darker sides framed the platinum blond on top, making it appear even whiter. It fell over my left eye and with a little snip at the back, a little sticky spray to spike up the area around the crown, and I'd look like "Oh my God, oh my God, oh my God! Xandir P. Wifflebottom!"

I was a nerdy game- and adventure-loving cartoon superhero.

The stylist obviously had watched Drawn Together as well because he started pointing and laughing until he had tears rolling down his face. By the time I left the salon, I wasn't looking much like Charlie Chaplin, but the top could probably be slicked back or hidden under Chaplin's signature derby, if not, I'd cut it when I got back from my trip.

Standing in front of the large mirror in the bathroom of my hotel room, I took in my wild new haircut, the dramatic smoky eye shadow, smooth skin, and flawlessly lined and painted lips, and I looked nothing like a cartoon. I looked fabulous, if I did say so myself. The clothing I picked for the club was also nothing like that of an animated superhero sidekick.

Teal silk T-shirt that hugged my lean body like a second skin, straight jeans, and a pair of Dr. Martens Drake shoes. I was also accessorized to the T with rhinestone belt, numerous bracelets on both wrists, and a simple silver cross pendant around my neck.

All the confidence I had in my looks plummeted to my knees, along with everything else, when there was a knock on the door. I was literally shaking, forcing my feet to move unsteadily toward the door.

My hand perched on the knob, I shuddered when a trickle of perspiration ran down my spine. *C'mon, Danny, this is not about you. This is Bo's night. Man up, bitch!*

I took a deep breath, mentally flipped off the irritating little fucker in my head, and opened the door.

It was only Bo.

"Danny!" Bo hugged me tightly and patted me on the back before stepping into the room. "Damn, you look good!"

"Thanks." I peered out into the hall but there was no one there. I shut the door, relieved? Disappointed? "Of course I do." I waved a limp-wristed hand at him. "You say that like it's a surprise."

"Whatever," he said and slumped back in one of the leather club chairs. "God, I need a drink and maybe some coffee. I'm exhausted."

"Katie running you a little ragged, is she?" I asked and took the other club chair next to him.

"You have no idea! I'll be glad when this is over. Here." He held out a folded piece of paper.

"What is it," I asked, taking the paper.

"Rules."

"What! You're kidding me, right?" I smoothed open the note.

"She made me promise I'd give it to you." He shrugged. "She'll ask you about it I'm sure."

1. Have him in his tux and at the church by two

2. No

I crumbled it into a ball and threw it behind me. "I'll follow rule one and deliver you to the church on time, but other than that, she don't get to make no stinking rules until she has that ring on your finger."

We high-fived and both laughed.

"So umm…." I tapped my finger against the arm of the chair. "Is it going to be just us?"

"He's waiting in the lobby. He knows we haven't seen each other in a while and wanted to give us some time to catch up."

"That's stupid."

"I know. I told him it wasn't necessary, 'cause we're like two high school girls with new phones with the amount of texting and calling we do. I haven't seen him look this bad since—"

I held up a hand. "Don't say it. Tonight is about you. I promise I'll behave and make him feel comfortable. I don't plan on bringing up anything from the past. Not tonight."

Bo looked at me skeptically. "You really think that's possible?"

No. Lance wasn't the only one nervous as hell. I was fucking petrified to see him. "Sure!" I said with a confidence I didn't feel. I went to my feet and held out my hand. "C'mon, let's go get your future brother-in-law, get you a stiff drink, and find a couple of strippers to give you a stiffie."

He laughed, allowed me to pull him to his feet, and draped an arm around my shoulders. "That was rule number two."

"Pfft! Don't get all pussy-whipped on me now. Save that shit for when she attaches your ball and chain." I grabbed the key card from the dresser as we walked by and shoved it in my back pocket with my wallet. "Tonight, the only rule we have is we must have fun in whatever we do." I opened the door and ushered him out with a wave of my arm. I followed him down the hall, hoping like hell I would be able to follow my own rule.

Lance was standing with his back to us when we walked into the lobby, looking out the large front window. My heart recognized him immediately and skipped a beat. He was broader, his black T-shirt stretched tight over his wide back and thick biceps. I remembered he'd always had large, well-developed thighs but now they were like thick tree trunks. Obviously the NFL worked him hard—he was huge.

I hadn't even realized my feet and my breath had stopped as surely as my heart until Bo nudged me.

"You okay?" he whispered.

My throat had gone dry and constricted, making it impossible to respond, but I nodded. *I can do this,* I chanted over and over in my head, and forced my feet to move. My force of will over my limbs was stripped away when Lance turned, a slight smile on his lips, making me wonder if he'd been watching my approach in the dark glass, and those extraordinary gray eyes met mine.

"Hi, Danny."

In the blink of an eye I was transported back to the last time I'd seen him. To the moment when I knew beyond a shadow of a doubt that I loved him and the surety that I'd be devastated when I walked away.

Had it not been for Bo standing next to me, the night before he was to marry, I would have turned around and run like hell. I didn't want to feel that pain again, yet I could already feel it creeping down my spine, seeping its way into my soul.

But it *was* about Bo, and with an inner strength I had no idea I possessed, I plastered on a warm smile and said, "Hi, Lance, you ready to party?" I didn't dare extend my hand to shake his or move any closer to him. No way could I touch him. I was a tough bastard, a damn good actor, but there were limits to what I could endure.

I don't know what Bo was expecting me to say or do, but he visibly slumped in relief next to me. "Hell yeah, I need a drink."

"Same here," Lance responded.

I locked my arm in Bo's—more to hold myself up, my legs were shaking so bad—and led him to the door. I could feel Lance's eyes on me, boring into my back, and I had to clamp down on my muscles to stop the shiver that threatened.

Although the sun had set, the heat of the late July day hadn't yet cooled. It was only a short walk to Jamin's but sweat had broken out on my brow by the time we made it to the club. I was the first to hand the bouncer my ID and waited just inside the door as Bo and Lance followed suit. I got a chance to study Lance without him knowing it. The sweat on his brow and thick neck glistened on his tanned skin. His hair was longer, much the same style it had been during the time we had been snowed in together. I couldn't help but remember what he looked like that night, the sweat on his skin from the exertion and pleasure, rather than the heat of the day, as we rubbed our bodies together. The way he'd rolled me over, eyes twinkling and a huge smile on his face when he asked if we could do it again.

Christ, it was going to be a long night if every movement he made, even sweat on his brow, reminded me of the past.

I forced myself to turn away and take in the club around me.

Jamin's was hopping, but it wasn't packed—only about three-fourths of the tables had patrons sitting at them. The bar against the far wall had a few open stools and no one in line waiting for a drink. The multicolored lights on the ceiling flickered and blinked in time to the techno dance mix blasting from hidden speakers.

Jamin's didn't have a dance floor—tables filled every open surface of floor—but there was a small stage on the opposite wall from the bar designed for dancing of the provocative kind. A pretty girl with long, brunette wavy hair danced seductively in nothing but black, spiked-heel, knee-high boots, black lace thong, and black lace push-up bra.

It wasn't my kind of show, wrong plumbing, but Bo would love it. I spotted a free table and beckoned them to follow me. I figured while Lance and Bo stuck crumpled dollar bills in the stripper's G-strings, I could dampen my senses with hard liquor.

After an hour, I was on my second Jack and Coke and Lance was quietly sipping on his beer, the both of us both trying to discreetly look at the other. Bo was sitting stiffly, nursing his original screwdriver. I knew I had to do something or Bo's bachelor party was going to be a bust.

I excused myself and made my way to the bar.

"What can I get you?"

"Three shots of tequila, three Miller drafts, and a lap dance for my buddy who is saying 'I do' tomorrow."

"I can get you the drinks but you have to talk to Miss Melanie about the dance." He pointed toward the end of the bar to a heavyset, middle-aged woman with a high blonde wig, heavy makeup smeared on her wrinkled face, and her large breasts practically spilling out of her corset. *Lovely,* I thought sarcastically.

"Be right back," I told him with a smile and headed to the end of the bar.

"Miss Melanie," I said, holding out my hand.

She took my hand and I brought her pudgy paw to my mouth and kissed it. "I'd like to hire one of your beautiful girls to entertain my friend."

"Well, ain't you just a sweet talker." Her eyes roamed down my body, leisurely making my skin crawl. *Eww!* "Quite the looker too. You ever do any stripping?"

"Only in private." I winked at her and she laughed.

"For you, twenty bucks for a public show, a hundred if you want one of those 'only in private' shows."

"Public is fine." I pulled a twenty out of my wallet and handed it to her. Miss Melanie didn't take it but jiggled her boobs. Good God. The things I had to do for a friend. I tucked the twenty in her cleavage and pointed out Bo, thanked her, and picked up our drinks before heading back to the table.

BO SAT on a straight-back chair in the middle of the stage, legs sprawled out as a tall, lean blonde straddled his thighs, gyrating and grinding against his crotch. Even from where I was sitting, I could see the sweat rolling down his temples as he gritted his teeth and did his damnedest not to grind back. He was so going to kill me.

Was Lance getting off on the show? Was he remembering his first stripper experience or was that fantasy behind him? I stole a glance in his direction, eyes landing on his crotch and the thick bulge in his jeans. Definitely enjoying the show. When I looked up, he wasn't watching the show but staring intently at me.

The crowd around us was screaming and hooting as the show continued, the music blaring, making it impossible to hear each other. Lance leaned in, my breath hitched when his warm breath tickled my ear.

"Life has been good to you. You look amazing."

I shuddered at his heat and scent surrounding me. "I could say the same to you."

He chuckled but it sounded kind of sad. "You have no idea."

What did he mean? Had life been good to him the past three years? He had achieved his goals. He looked amazing, better than I remembered. How could he not think life was good?

We sat there close, and I swore I could hear him inhaling deeply. Maybe I only felt it, but his nearness was doing something to me none of these half-naked women could do. My mouth felt like the Sahara, tongue dry and throat gritty. He still could affect me like no one ever had. I picked up my beer and took a sip, my hand shaking so badly the contents sloshed over the sides and landed on my thighs as I set it back on the table. I wiped at it absently, cheeks heating.

Lance leaned back only slightly, but his eyes instantly went to the hand I had on my thigh. He licked his lips and when he looked back up, his eyes were heavy-lidded.

This had been a really, really bad idea.

I gestured toward the stage, where the stripper had turned and was now straddling Bo in the opposite direction, her firm ass swaying only inches from Bo's bright red face. "He appears to be enjoying the show."

Lance cast a quick glance at the stage then back at me. "Katie would kill him if she saw this."

"Yeah, well, I'm not going to tell her. What happens tonight stays between the three of us."

He nodded and took a big gulp of his beer, and then moved his chair closer until our thighs were touching. He draped an arm over the back of my chair, our heads only an inch apart. "You like living in New York?"

"Uh… yeah." I nodded toward the stage again. "Hot blonde bimbo is dry-fucking Bo and you want to talk about New York?"

"I'm just curious how you've been."

"Now?"

"You're a lot more interesting than what's happening up there. A lot hotter too."

Please, please, please don't do this! Please don't say things like that, I begged him silently. I knew if he kept up this line of conversation, I'd end up doing things that I would regret by the time this weekend was over. I needed to steer this conversation away from me.

"New York is great. I hear you were drafted by Minnesota. You like it there?"

"It's okay." He shrugged.

The crowd got even louder; the group of guys at the table to our right went to their feet and screamed while waving dollars. On the stage, the blonde had been joined by two other women, one redhead and one brunette. Bo was now on his feet, his shirt open, arms thrown around the blonde and the redhead as they moved him toward the stairs. He looked blissed out. The brunette was moving down the stairs, no doubt to work the crowd. From the reaction of the drunk boys next to us, she was in for a rowdy time.

"Looks like Bo liked it up there!"

Lance sat back in his chair, but he didn't move it away from mine. "Yup, better order that boy a shot."

The strippers plopped Bo down in the chair back at our table and they each kissed him on the cheek. He popped one on the bare butt as she moved away, making her squeal. "Drinks on me!" he yelled, and I rolled my eyes at him.

"Down, tiger! Katie will rip your balls off if you spend your honeymoon money. Here, start with this." I handed him the last shot of tequila and got the attention of a waitress.

It took three hours, another lap dance, and hiding Bo's wallet before he finally laid his head down on the table and tapped out. Through it all I was painfully aware of Lance sitting next to me, felt his eyes on me the entire time, and I was a fucking mess. I hadn't had any more to drink, switching to Coke, knowing I'd have to help Bo back to the hotel room. It was the most excruciating three hours of my life.

Lance was right there. All I had to do was reach out and grab him. Pull him to me and press our mouths together. The look in his eyes said he'd welcome it. The attraction between us was arcing and flashing like lightning, growing in intensity with each passing moment. The air around us sizzled with electricity. Fuck, I wanted him. I wanted him so bad every cell in my body ached with the need. Only the pressure in my chest, the viselike grip around my heart, held me back.

Lance and I on either side of Bo, we finally pulled him to his feet and got him out the door. The cool air of the night felt great on my skin; the quiet helped soothe my throbbing head—the one on my shoulders anyway. Neither of us said a word as we walked Bo—or rather, dragged him—back to the hotel and got him tucked into bed.

It wasn't until we had him settled that Lance turned those gray eyes on me and said, "Want to come to my room for a nightcap?"

Yes! "I'm not so sure that's a good idea," I told him reluctantly. "I'm not sure I could keep my hands off you if we were alone."

"What if I don't want you to keep your hands off me?" he asked, moving closer into my personal space and crowding as he looked down at me.

I swallowed hard. "Lance, I don't think—"

He reached up and brushed the back of his knuckles gently along my jaw. "I've missed you. I told myself I wouldn't do this, that I could handle being in the same room with you and not touch you. But I can't. I've missed you so fucking much, Danny. There hasn't been a day since you walked out of my life that I haven't thought about you."

I leaned into his touch, even knowing I shouldn't. If I were smart, I'd ask him to leave, crawl into the empty bed, and put this night behind me. Tomorrow, after the ceremony, I'd never have to see Lance Lenard again.

"Please," he whispered. "I'm not going to push you into anything. At least come to my room, have one drink, and tell me about your life in New York. Tell me you're happy."

Smarts hadn't always been my strong point, at least not when it came to Lance. I turned away from him, grabbed my room key, stuffing it into my pocket. "Lead the way."

I was so fucked, both in a good way, and in a very, very, very bad way.

chapter
nineteen

I FOLLOWED Lance down the hall to his room. I was vibrating with excitement and arousal as I watched him move. Each step he took flexed those bulging muscles and made me tingle. My gut, however, wasn't getting with the program. It was rumbling and rolling, nausea threatening, but I kept moving. I hadn't ever been able to say no to Lance, and no amount of time apart had changed that.

Lance ran his key card in the lock and held open the door for me. He didn't move and I was forced to brush against him, intensifying the excitement.

"Make yourself at home," Lance said as he dropped his key and wallet on the dresser.

I took a seat in one of the club chairs—the bed seemed like a bad idea.

"What can I get you to drink? I've got soda, water, or we can crack open the bar."

"Water is fine."

Lance rummaged in the small fridge, pulled out two bottles of water, handing me one and taking the other, and sat in the chair next to me.

"I think Bo had a good time. I'm not so sure he'll remember it, but that's probably not a bad thing." Lance twisted open his bottle of water and took a long gulp. My eyes were drawn to his throat working and I squirmed in my seat.

I opened my own water and took a sip to wet my dry throat. "Yeah, I was a little worried at first it was going to be a bust, but I think he enjoyed himself."

"It was a little tense at first." He gave me a small smile. "I admit I was a little freaked out after seeing you."

"I have that effect on people," I said, trying to relieve some of the tension that seemed to hang in the air. "I'm kind of freaky."

"I wouldn't use that description," he murmured, bottle against his lips, and then tipped it up again.

"No? What description would you use?"

Lance stared down at the bottle in his hand, thumb rubbing across the condensation that dripped down the side. "Unforgettable," he finally said.

That had me chuckling. "I'm one of a kind, that's for damn sure."

"Yeah, you are," he said sincerely, gaze meeting mine.

The look in his eyes made me uncomfortable and I had to look away, the laughter dying in my throat.

"So tell me about Minnesota. What's it like playing ball there?"

"It's great, but I'm not too confident I'll be playing there much longer."

"How come?"

"Did some damage to my shoulder. They did their best to repair it, but it keeps dislocating. I spent the last year on the injured reserve list. Still not up to game-ready."

"Man, that sucks."

"One of the hazards of the job," he said wistfully.

I reached down and untied my boots, pulling them off and tucking my feet up under me. I sat facing him, picking at the label on my bottle. "So what are you going to do if you can't play ball?"

"I don't know. I have a few options. Trainer, maybe get into the recruiting department. I could see myself as a scout. Traveling the country and getting paid to watch the game."

"That still has to be tough. You worked so hard to get to the NFL. No Plan B, if I remember."

"Yeah, well, things change. I realize we can't always get what we want."

From the look Lance gave me, I couldn't help but think he wasn't talking about football.

"What about you, Danny? Did you get what you wanted?"

Not everything I wanted. "I haven't made it to Broadway yet, but I just signed on as the lead in a show off-Broadway."

"Yeah? What show?"

"You're looking at the infamous womanizer Charlie Chaplin, which I think is hilarious. But it's a great opportunity, and I've had some experience being a tramp."

I regretted the reference to Chaplin's famous role *The Tramp* the minute it was out of my mouth. Before Lance I had been a tramp; if it felt good, then I did it. I had no regrets, but for some ungodly weird reason, I didn't want him to know. Didn't want him to view me as a slut, or worse, shallow. Lance's face fell and he looked uncomfortable, shifting in his seat.

"What about you? You have anyone special in your life?"

He didn't look up, just stared at the now-empty bottle in his hands. "After you left, Morgan and I got back together."

That didn't surprise me. She would make the perfect football player's trophy wife. I just nodded in response and smiled even though my stomach was in knots. "That's good."

"Nah. It was never a good decision. I mean, I cared about her, but you can't build a relationship on settling for second best. I ended up resenting the hell out of her, and when it ended last year, it had gotten pretty ugly."

"From what I'd heard, she was crazy about you. What's to resent about that?"

Lance shot me a brief glance. "She wasn't you," he said softly and then returned his attention back to the bottle.

"Oh."

"Yeah, I was pretty messed up after you left."

Lance wasn't the only one who had been messed up. Hell, that first month after that last day with him had been a blur of pain and anger. It had gotten so bad that by the time I joined my parents in New York, I had no desire to return to Michigan. I had always wanted to attend CCNY but had gone with my second choice and stayed close to home. With my parents no longer living there, I had no reason to stay in Michigan and spent summer break transferring to NYC to continue my studies. I finally pulled my ass up out of that fucking misery and got on with my life, but Christ, it had been hard.

"I'm really sorry about running out on you like I did. I should have at least said good-bye."

He held up a hand. "Don't be. When you first left, I was so fucking mad at you. Hated you for what you had done. Blamed you for the attraction, the rumors, the embarrassment, the pain, frustration, all of it was your fault. I had to tell someone, and the only person I could tell was Katie. I poured my heart out to her, and I thought she would hate you too for what you did to me. And if she hated you, then you would lose Bo, and I figured it would serve you right.

"Only she didn't. It took a lot of screaming and yelling but I finally figured out I'd been the idiot." Lance shook his head and looked at me with a self-deprecating grin. "My sister is notorious for handing me my ass."

That made me smile too, even though my chest was aching. "Yeah, I've seen her in action."

"Anyway, she made me realize that I was the one to blame for my pain, that I had created it and had to own it. It was unfair for me to keep you in my life but never acknowledge to anyone that you were there. I get that now. But it took some time. At first, I honestly believed that I could go back to the way my life was before I met you." He shrugged. "Well, I already told you how that turned out." Lance tossed his bottle, hitting the garbage can on the other side of the room. "Sorry about laying that shit on you. You didn't need to hear about my screwed-up life." He laughed without mirth. "I hear yours is going well. You've been with that dancer for quite a while. Kyle, isn't it?"

I did need to hear it, and I don't know why—maybe I'm a sick bastard—but knowing he had been hurting as badly as I had been when it ended did in some kind of twisted way make me feel better. However, I didn't think it would do either of us any good to add to his guilt by telling him how far I fell after I left. Yup, totally a sick bastard, since I was delighted that he'd also been keeping tabs on me and had known about Kyle.

"Yes, Kyle. He's a dancer with a troupe based out of Chicago."

"That has to be hard," he murmured. "Maintaining a long-distance relationship. I know it was hard on Morgan."

"It was. I had an opportunity to take a role in Chicago to be with him, but I belong in New York. Since neither of us was willing to give up our dream, we agreed to go our separate ways when I took the Chaplin role."

"Sorry to hear that."

I tilted my head and studied him. "Are you really?"

He held my gaze for long moments. He moved from his chair, going to his knees next to me, and took my hand in his. "No."

Warmth spread out from where he held my hand, traveling up my arm like an electric current. My pulse increased, and without conscious thought, I was leaning toward him. When our mouths pressed together, it was slow and hesitant, a test of how far I would let him go. It felt so good to feel his lips against mine, feel his breath against my flesh, in that moment that I would have let him go as deep and as far as he wanted, and I melted against him.

Lance moved his free hand to the back of my head, pulling me closer and deepening the kiss. I felt sparks across my tongue as his flavor filled my mouth, and I hummed. I pulled my hand free from his and clutched at the cotton covering his chest. I could feel the tight muscles flexing beneath my knuckles.

"I've missed you so much," he whispered against my mouth, licking and nipping at my bottom lip like it was a succulent dessert he couldn't get enough of, searching for more flavor. "Never stopped."

"I know." But I couldn't say any more because he was exploring my mouth again. Pressing close, he clenched his hand in my hair as if he wanted to crawl inside me. And oh, sweet Jesus, I wanted him there and I wanted to be within him. I wanted to wrap myself inside him.

Make him my cocoon and hide from the past, the present, and the future. When he was kissing me, the world ceased to exist and everything seemed so easy, so right.

The kiss went on and on and on, neither of us wanting it to end. Even as my lungs screamed for air, I couldn't stop. I had three years of missed kisses I was trying to make up for in one prolonged kiss. I roamed and massaged across his chest, over his shoulders, and down the sinew along his spine. He was so much bigger than I remembered, foreign and yet so familiar.

When we were finally forced apart, we both panted into each other's mouth, our eyes locked. I pulled his sweet breath in to my lungs and fed him mine back.

Lance lifted me from the chair, encouraging me to hold on to him as he walked us over to the bed, placing soft kisses to my lips, cheeks, and jaw the entire way. He lowered me onto the bed and followed. I spread my legs wide, giving him the extra room his big frame needed as he covered my body with his.

All thoughts except the feel of Lance's body against mine fled. He nuzzled my neck, searching for his spot, and when his lips found it, he began to suck. I cried out, my moans growing in intensity as he marked me and pressed his hard cock against mine. I was awash in sensation, humping and jerking. My body knew his intimately, and it responded without any conscious thought on my part. It was as if we had never been apart, our hands seeking out each sensitive spot on the other's body as we reacquainted ourselves with each favorite area. A bony hip, the soft area below an armpit, small of a back, and all the while Lance continued to suck at my neck in his spot, leaving his mark of possession.

My mind had short-circuited, and everything narrowed down to the physical sensations surging through my body. It became pure animal instinct to hump against him, our cocks smashed together and throbbing. The smell, the feel of bulging and straining muscles, and I was so fucking ready. I wanted him like I'd never wanted anyone. Had it stayed an instinct, simply an animal's need to rut, I have no doubt I would have ripped his clothes from his body and let him fuck me right then and there.

However, it wasn't about carnal desires when he cupped my cheek, his thumb rubbing at the corner of my mouth. "Tell me you missed me too. That I wasn't the only one who felt it."

It was like a bucket of ice water was splashed on me. Where only seconds before I was pulling him to me, I was now shoving him away and scrambling out from under him.

"Danny, what is it? What did I say?" he asked, voice unsure.

I ran a hand through my hair and began to pace. "Yeah, I missed you, Lance. Nearly every fucking day."

"Then I don't understand. What's wrong?"

"Because I don't want to go back there again."

Lance moved to the edge of the bed, elbows on his knees, and hung his head in his hands. "You've moved on," he said quietly.

"I had to!" The words came out harsh, panic making them crack. I had almost let myself fall right back into his arms, his charms, and I couldn't—no, I *wouldn't* go back to that ugly place I was three years ago.

"You say I don't know what my leaving did to you? Well you don't know the fucking hell I went through either. I dropped out of school. I lay in my parents' spare room for a month, not interested in anything but staring at the ceiling or sleeping and trying not to cry my fucking eyes out. Trying not to love you!"

I froze and clamped my hand over my mouth. I hadn't wanted to admit that, not to him. When Lance stood up and started to come toward me, I spun away and turned my back to him, my heart like a jackhammer in my chest. *Run! Get out of this room before you say another word. Run and don't look back.* Go!

Before I could get my feet to obey the little voice in my head, Lance wrapped his arms around me from behind and held me tight against him. He wasn't going to let me run this time. "It didn't go away, did it?"

Tears burned at the back of my eyes, but I blinked them away, stubbornly refusing to let them spill. "No," I whispered dejectedly.

"Thank God." He squeezed me tighter. His mouth was only an inch from my ear when he said, "I never stopped loving you either."

I struggled to pull free. I needed to get the hell away from him before I heard another word. Before my heart heard it and accepted it, because I knew it would be shattered all over again when I left. "Let me go."

Lance hesitated.

"I mean it. Turn me loose, now!"

I felt his reluctance, but he finally released me and I stepped away. I didn't turn to look at him. I didn't dare. "Why are you thanking God?" I asked, but I didn't take a step, afraid to move, afraid not to.

"I just found out that the man I've been in love with for three years loves me back. Why wouldn't I be thankful?"

That got me moving, and I spun and glared at him. "Are you a fucking sadist?"

"Uh, no."

"You must be! Knowing that we're in love makes it worse."

"I don't—"

"Are you going to tell your teammates you're in love with a guy?"

Lance's gaze fell away from mine, and I knew the answer. It just fueled my rage. Not just at him, but at myself as well, at the whole fucked-up situation.

"Are you going to tell your parents you're gay? Your friends?" I clenched my hands into fists and screamed, "Are you going to give up football, your home, everything, and move to New York to be with me?"

He hung his head and stumbled back, sitting hard on the bed.

"I like my life in New York, and I have no plans to leave. I like that all my friends, the people I work with, the chick at the coffee shop on the corner, and the goddamn kid at McDonald's all knew I was gay because my ex-boyfriend wasn't afraid to hold my hand in public. Would you be that brave?"

Silence.

"You still thanking God there, Lance? Does knowing I'm in love with you, knowing how much this is fucking killing me, how much it's going to hurt you when I walk away again, make you feel better?"

I knew I wouldn't be able to hold back the tears that were pooling in my eyes much longer. I grabbed my boots, moved to the door, and opened it. Just like the last time, I was leaving him all alone in a small hotel room, running away before my tears could roll down my face. The only difference was this time, he knew I was leaving.

I stepped out the door, stopping at the last minute to say, "I don't thank God. I'm cursing him."

CHAPTER
TWENTY

BO AND Katie said their vows before their families and a few close friends in the backyard of her parents' home. The July day was warm, the azure-blue sky cloudless, and the sun shone down on Katie's bare shoulders, her simple white dress glistening in the bright rays. However, it was the glow from within that truly made her shine. It was the same kind of radiance that emitted from Bo when he slipped a simple gold band on her left hand. I had never seen him so happy.

The yard had been decorated with white bows tied to the ends of each row of chairs, and a white paper walkway strewn with tiny purple flowers that matched the bouquet in Katie's hands. From all appearances, it was the traditional summer wedding with only two exceptions. Katie had chosen Lance to stand with her—no bridesmaids or maid of honor, just her best friend and twin. The other exception was Bo had a best man who looked like a cartoon sidekick, but I sacrificed the makeup, and I still rocked the black tux. There was a third exception, but the tension arcing between the best man and the man of honor was well hidden. I doubted anyone except for Lance and me knew how hard it was for the two of us to be standing there, less than ten feet apart.

After I had left Lance's room the night before, I crawled into bed with Bo. He stunk of the alcohol he'd consumed, but I didn't notice, just as he didn't notice my tears. I was surprised that I had been able to sleep. Maybe it was that my brain just shut down from the overload, and I woke up feeling raw. My eyes felt like the inside of my lids had been scrubbed with sandpaper and they were swollen and puffy. I still looked better than Bo had.

He'd stumbled out of bed and I heard him groan when he saw his reflection in the mirror. Large, dark bags hung under his eyes, his complexion pale, and he was visibly shaking. "This is your fault!" he called out from the bathroom.

I pulled myself out of bed and leaned against the doorjamb to the bathroom. "Actually the drinking was your fault, but I'll take credit for the hickey on your ass."

"What!"

I laughed when Bo twisted and went up on tiptoes trying to see his ass in the mirror.

"I'm just kidding. Get your ass in the shower, you stink."

"Fucker. I'm supposed to be getting married today, and thanks to you I'm going to be puking and passing out at the altar."

"You'll be fine. A little coffee, a little breakfast, and you'll be good as new."

He stepped into the shower and looked at me skeptically, but I had been right. I drove him to the church in my rental car, Lance following in Bo's car—a small blessing—and had him dressed and ready to say his vows with time to spare. No puking or passing out was involved, just lots of water and a handful of aspirin beforehand.

"I now pronounce you husband and wife. You may kiss the bride."

Bo pulled Katie into his arms and kissed her to the cheers and applause of the crowd.

It was tense following Bo and Katie back down the aisle with Lance walking next to me, but we made it. I'd be heading back to my life in less than twenty-four hours. The only thing left to endure was a small lunch, a couple of toasts. Two hours max, since the newlyweds had a flight to catch, and I could spend the rest of the evening licking my wounds and packing for my trip back home.

My stomach was so knotted up that I couldn't eat much, so I sat there playing with my food with a fake smile on my face while family and friends walked by the table congratulating the happy couple. I snuck a glance in Lance's direction, and he wasn't hiding it as well as I was. He looked as miserable as I felt.

With lunch finished, I stood, grabbed my champagne glass, and cleared my throat. "Everyone, if I could get your attention. I'd like to say a few words.

"For those of you who may not know me, my name is Danny, and I have the great fortune of being Bo's best friend since we were thirteen. As you can imagine, we are as different as night and day. When we were younger, I was the one prancing around pretending I was Fred Astaire, and he had his nose in a book. But no matter our differences, we were always there for each other. In fact, together we survived the teenage years, went to university together, and were dormmates. Throughout our lives, most of our firsts were experienced together. First day of high school, first heartbreak, first detention." I looked over at Bo's mom and smiled. "Don't ask."

She just shook her head and laughed.

"In fact, due to a little payback I owed Bo for attending a ballet, I was with him when he asked Katie out for the first time. I'm going to miss being there for the rest of the *firsts* in your life, but I'm glad you have Katie to experience them with you. Marriage is not about finding a person you can live with, it's about finding the person you can't live without."

I raised my glass to Bo and Katie. "My friend has found that person."

I took a sip of my champagne and accepted hugs from Bo and Katie as everyone clapped, and then slumped back in my chair.

One more speech.

Lance stood and picked up his glass. "When Katie asked me to stand up with her, I thought it was a little odd since I don't look like your typical maid of honor. But the more I thought about it, it made perfect sense. Being twins, we started life together, so it's only natural that I be standing next to her when she starts her new life. It's crazy. It seems like just yesterday she was pestering me to borrow my bike, complaining about me leaving my smelly equipment laying around the house, and I was threatening my teammates if they went anywhere near her.

"Katie and I have always been very close. We both knew from a young age where we were going in life. I was going to be an NFL star and she was going to be some nerdy CEO, never be tied down, and travel the world. Throughout our lives, we encouraged each other. There was no stopping either of us. We could do anything we set our minds to, there were no alternate plans, and we didn't need them.

"Then Katie met Bo. I have never seen my sister happier since the day she met him, and I know they will have an amazing life together." Lance kept his eyes on me, like he was peering right into me. "She and Bo are proof that carefully laid plans aren't always the best. Sometimes Plan B is the real dream come true."

I sat there trembling as he continued. Could it be possible that he was talking about us? Did I dare hope he was?

Lance raised his glass. "Here's to my amazing sister and her new husband. Reality is finally better than your dreams."

I could barely get the small sip of champagne down, my throat was so constricted, but I toasted my best friend and his new wife. The way Lance had looked at me and his words played on a continuous loop in my brain, until I thought I would go mad with trying to figure out what they meant.

AS SOON as the last speech was given and Bo and Katie rushed off, I said my good-byes. I was disappointed that Lance had seemed to disappear into the crowd of family, and I walked out to my car without saying good-bye to him.

But I hadn't needed to worry about it. I found him leaning against the driver's side door of my car, arms and ankles crossed, head tipped back, looking up at the cloudless sky. My stomach fluttered when I spotted him. He looked so amazing in his tuxedo and I knew it was an image I'd keep with me forever.

As soon as he spotted me walking toward him, he straightened. "I was wondering when the masses of aunts and grandparents were going to let you go. How're your cheeks?"

I smiled and rubbed at my right cheek. "Pinched out."

"Nice speech you gave."

"Thanks, yours was great too." I stopped a couple of feet away from him. "You heading back to Minnesota tonight?"

"Nope."

I couldn't see his eyes through the dark glass of his shades, but I just knew he was staring at me. I shifted from foot to foot, my keys jingling in my hand. "Me neither. I'm heading back tomorrow. To New York, not Minnesota."

"You going back to the hotel now?"

"I had planned on it."

In one deft move, Lance plucked the keys from my hand. "Cool, I'll drive." He moved around the car, hit the key fob, disengaging the lock, and opened the passenger door.

"I don't think that's a good idea, do you?"

"Sure it is," he said confidently. "I have a few things I need your advice on."

"You can't ask me here?" But I was already walking around to the passenger side of the car. My head may not have figured it out yet, but my body already knew I'd go with him and was moving.

"Nope. This may take a while."

"All right." I slid into the car. Lance shut the door and ran around to the driver's side.

As soon as he had us on the road, he said, "For such a short notice, their wedding turned out great."

"Yeah, it did. Is that what you want to talk about? How nice Bo and Katie's wedding was?"

"No, but I figured the important stuff should be done face to face." He glanced at me "Don't you think?"

I shrugged. So for the thirty-minute ride, we talked about their wedding, their honeymoon, and everything but what he deemed as the *important* stuff. I was a nervous wreck the entire way, both excited about hearing what he wanted to tell me and dreading it. The last conversation had been hell and I didn't think I could handle another one so soon.

Dreading or not, the minute we got into my hotel room, I shrugged out of my coat, throwing it on the bed. "Okay, talk."

"Nothing like getting right to it, huh?"

"I'd say chatting about flower arrangements, wedding vows, and your aunt Silvia for the last half hour allows me to be a little demanding."

I shucked off the rest of the more cumbersome pieces of my outfit until I was wearing just the pants and white shirt. My socks and shoes were thrown to the floor with the rest of the pieces, and I crawled up into the center of the king-size bed and sat back against the headboard.

Lance followed suit and joined me on the bed. "See, I had a lot of time to think about what you said after you left. Well, after I dealt with how I felt about you leaving. That part sucked, but that's what got me thinking."

"I said a lot of things to you last night."

"Yeah, I know." He took my hand and entwined our fingers. "That part about cursing God for loving each other, that was really messed up."

"That's how I feel."

"I know, and that's just not right. Loving someone isn't supposed to hurt this bad. I mean, it'd be one thing if something had happened to the person you loved and they were gone forever. But to know they are out there, feeling the same way you are and being just as miserable because you're not together—well, that just doesn't make any sense. It's just stupid."

"Death isn't the only thing that can keep people apart."

Lance brought my hand to his mouth and kissed my knuckles. "Like stupid jocks who don't have a Plan B."

Sometimes Plan B is the real dream come true. "Do you have one now?"

"Yeah, I do." Lance took our joined hands and ran them down my cheek. "I want to be as happy as my sister and Bo are. I can only do that if I have you in my life. You're my Plan B, Danny."

"But—"

He silenced me with a tender kiss. "I'd be lying if I said I wasn't scared, because I am. I don't know if I am as brave as you are or your friends. But I'm done being miserable. I'm done missing you and wondering where you are. Driving myself crazy wondering who you're with." He brushed his lips against mine and spoke with our flesh touching. "I do know that I love you, all the rest is just details."

My heart nearly burst out of my chest I was so happy to hear him say those words. I was both laughing and crying when I climbed on top of him and straddled his lap. I cupped his face in my hands and met those extraordinary eyes. "It's about fucking time."

Our mouths came together in a possessive and fierce kiss. Both of us trying to take control of it, yet not really caring who did as tongues dueled and teeth clashed. Lance's arms were around me and he was moving down the bed, stretching out. It was difficult and awkward, neither of us wanting to break away from the kiss. Somehow we managed to move into the same position we'd been the night before: lips-to-lips, chest-to-chest, and groin-to-groin. Only this time it was me on top, lying between Lance's spread legs, and I had no plans on stopping until I had tasted and touched every inch of him.

Hands roamed freely, wandering over chests and down arms and backs. All the while our lips were fused together. He was like my air and I couldn't pull my mouth from his. I somehow managed to get his shirt unbuttoned and pulled from the waistband of his pants. Impatient to feel him against me with nothing between us, I broke the kiss only long enough to yank my partially unbuttoned shirt over my head and kissed him again.

Lance moaned huskily the minute our bare chests came in contact, and his arms were around me again, pressing me hard against his broad chest as he massaged and kneaded my back. I could feel the damp hairs on his chest tickling against my nipples. My cock pressed against his, hardening further with each pulse and the press of Lance's rocking hips.

I licked up the length of his neck, teasing the lobe of his ear with my teeth. "You feel so good against me." I reached between us and popped the button on his slacks. "But I need to feel all of you."

Lance just nodded, his hands going to my pants and following my lead. Once he had my button undone and the zipper down, I leaned back long enough to shove them down my legs and off. I kissed the dark line of hair below his navel, then grabbed the waistband of both his slacks and boxers and pushed them down his legs.

Before I could toss them to the floor, Lance stopped me. "Wait, front pocket."

I searched his pocket, finding a condom and small packet of lube. I arched a brow at him. "You came prepared."

"Yeah, I had a new plan to work on."

"I think I'm going to like this new plan." My eyes were drawn to Lance's thick cock, hard and straining toward his stomach. I'd had an untold number of fantasies about that thick, beautiful cock buried deep inside me since I'd first met him, and my body vibrated with excitement at finally being able to fulfill that fantasy. I ran my hand up his thigh, to his groin, my fingers just barely brushing against his shaft, causing it to twitch. I looked up at him from under my lashes. "On second thought, I think I'm going to love this new plan."

Lance's eyes were heavy on me, watching my every move as I carefully tore open the foil package and pulled out the condom. I grasped the base of his cock, lifting it up and away from his body. He stopped my movements by laying a hand over mine.

"No. Want to feel you inside me."

I froze. "What?"

"I want you to fuck me, Danny."

My dick jerked. At least part of my body was screaming *Oh, hell yeah!* But another part of me wasn't so sure. The thought of being Lance's first thrilled me, but I remembered my first time and it hurt like a son of a bitch. I wasn't saying no, I just wanted it to be about mutual pleasure, not pain. He'd have plenty of time to explore that carnal delight, but not at that moment.

I shook my head. "Not this time. I don't want to hurt you."

"You won't." He sat up and took the condom from me. "I've been practicing."

"The hell you have!"

"I think about it all the time. Three years, Danny." Lance licked his palm then grasped my dick and pumped it a couple of times as I arched into his touch. I was so hard a steady flow of precum poured from the slit, mingling with the saliva on Lance's hand.

"Drove me crazy just thinking about fucking you, you fucking me." He leaned in and spoke quietly and seductively against my ear as he rolled the condom down my length. "I bought some toys."

The thought of Lance lying in his bed, fucking himself with a dildo and thinking of me, made my cock surge and swell even further and I could have come right there, but I held back. I wanted to be buried deep inside him before I did.

I looked down. Lance's big dick waved between us, looking ready and willing. I didn't know which I wanted more—to throw him back and pound into him, or throw him down and ride the fuck out of him. Either way, it was going to be hard and fast and I needed to know for sure. "You better not be fucking with me, Lance. I don't know if I could be gentle right now and I want to make this good for you."

Something wet landed in my hand and I looked down to see Lance squeezing out a generous amount of lube into my palm. His eyes were dark and heavy-lidded with lust, and they never left mine as he lay back and pulled his knees up, exposing his tight hole in invitation. I had my answer.

I rubbed my hands together, warming the cool gel, and then swiped a slick finger across his hole, working it in circles, teasing him open, and then worked one finger inside him, the muscles clamping down hard around the invader. Lance hissed.

"Fuck, but you're tight. You sure you've done this?"

Lance panted, big chest heaving. "Yeah, just go slow at first, okay?"

I kept working that one finger in and out, slowly and deeply initially, then faster. I kept my eyes on him, watching for any signs that I was hurting him, but he was watching me with hungry eyes and his fat cock was heavy and leaking on his stomach. He wanted this and goddamn I wanted to give it. I worked a second finger in along the first, stretching, curling, and twisting until I could work in a third.

Lance was groaning, his hips rocking, big body begging for more. "Danny." His voice was thick like he'd reached his limit and that was okay, because I'd reached mine too. Lance whimpered when I pulled my fingers from his ass, but I didn't leave him empty and needing for long.

I went up on my knee, grabbed my sheathed cock and guided it until the head was pressed against his tight bud. His muscles resisted at first but I kept up a steady pressure, and when the head of my cock finally pushed past the resistance and entered him, Lance's head lolled back and he moaned, my name barely recognizable his voice was so thick.

I shuddered, the walls of his passage clamping down hard on my cock, and I gritted my teeth, sliding deep until I felt my balls press snug against his ass. I froze, dick tingling and wanting to explode. "Oh, fuck me, you feel good."

Lance's face was flushed, those gray eyes like lasers boring into me. "That's next time, now fuck me!"

I pulled back until just the head was inside him and then thrust deep, bottoming out. I set a brutal rhythm, both of us beyond gentle and soft. Lance was so big and so fucking strong, I knew he could take it. I pushed his thighs back further and pounded into the hot, tight heat.

As soon as I changed my angle, Lance screamed, "Right there! Oh fuck, Danny. Right fucking there! Don't stop."

"Not gonna," I slurred.

The sound of our bodies slapping together, grunts, and low howls filled the room, and I wanted to weep with how perfect and right it felt.

I hunched over him, curling my body so I could take Lance's mouth. The kiss was awkward and sloppy as we both panted into it. Sweat was running down my spine, trickling from my temples, and my muscles trembled from the exertion, but I felt as if I could go all night. I wanted nothing more than to stay surrounded by his heat and scent, buried deep within my lover's body. Never wanted it to end, but he felt so good, and Lance was begging for more and harder and I couldn't stop slamming into him, giving him everything he wanted and taking everything I needed.

I was so close that there was no way I could last much longer, and when I fell into bliss, I was taking him with me. I fucked him brutally, hard, my hand wrapped around his cock jerking him off in time with my thrusts.

Lance threaded a hand in my hair and jerked my head to the side, the minute his mouth touched his mark on the side of my neck, he grunted, sucked at my neck, and hot seed fountained over my fist. Lance's ass clamped down hard, squeezing my prick, and I couldn't hold back. I think I shouted out his name and "I love you" and "mine," but I can't be sure, because Lance was sucking my throat and he was tugging my hair and a hand was squeezing my ass and it was all just too fucking much and I was coming so hard I saw stars.

I soared, and when it was over, I didn't float back down all soft and willowy. I crash landed. The tension and fear melted out of me. The pain of the last three years was gone and I felt whole for the first time in a long time. I was in Lance's arms and he was murmuring against my ear how much he loved me and about Plan Bs, and I believed him. I didn't have a shred of doubt that my longing for him was over. On some level I knew he was mine and I was his, and everything made perfect sense.

I drifted off to sleep, or passed out, or maybe I just let go of everything and lost myself in being his.

EPILOGUE

PRODUCTION had come to a halt, and I was taking a much-needed break and going home for the holidays. It was going to be Danielle's first Christmas, and as I was her godfather, there was no way in hell I was going to miss that first. I had thought with Bo getting married that we'd no longer be as close as we had been growing up. I was wrong. I may not be there every day, but I was there when Danielle took her first breath, at her christening, and now I'd be there for her first Christmas. The special moments we still shared. And I had been right—like there was any doubt of that—Bo was an amazing dad. He hadn't even dropped her on her head once.

I stretched out on the couch, cup of coffee in my hand, and enjoyed my last quiet morning before I headed into the world of craziness, pinched cheeks, and squealing and busy baby. I picked up the folded newspaper from the coffee table and snapped it open.

The second I read the headlines, I jerked up, coffee spilling onto my bare chest. "Ow! Fuck! Ow!" I set the mug away and wiped frantically at the mess with my robe.

"What's the matter?" Lance asked, rushing into the room, eyes wild, in just a towel wrapped around his wet and dripping body. "What happened?"

"I spilled coffee on my chest. I'm fine."

"Christ, Danny, you scared the hell out of me."

I rolled my eyes at him. "You panic when I get a paper cut or stub my toe."

He sat next to me, leaned over, and kissed the angry red spot on my chest softly. "That's because the thought of anything marring this perfect body drives me insane."

I quirked a brow at him. "You mar me all the time."

"Those are love marks, which only enhance your perfection."

I swatted him upside his head playfully. "You're such a big sap."

"But I'm your sap."

I pressed a soft kiss to his lips. "Yes, you are." I started to reach for him, when I remembered the paper in my hand. I held it out to him. "Did you see this?"

Lance grabbed the paper; I read the headline again while he did.

Ex-NFL Star to Marry Partner on New Year's Eve

Lance's lips twitched into a cocky smile. "Cool! They called me a star." He tossed the paper on the coffee table. "That's more than they called me when I played."

I stared at him in disbelief. "That doesn't bother you?"

"Hell no," he said, snuggling further into my side, one of his hands going to my thigh, rubbing. "What, you jealous that I'm the one being called a star for a change?"

I couldn't believe how blasé he was about the headline. Lance had had a rough time coming out—his dad still hadn't completely accepted his son was gay, and he'd lost a few people he had thought were his friends. But over the last year and a half he'd become a lot more comfortable with people knowing he was gay. Living in the New York theater district helped. No one really paid much attention to two men holding hands while they walked down the street or hugged in public. My friends, family, and coworkers accepted him without question, which helped ease him into his new life, but it was still like living in a bubble. I had thought he'd freak with the whole world knowing.

"You don't care that it's public knowledge that you're marrying a dude?"

"I think the fact that I got down on one knee in front of the theater on closing night pretty much guaranteed it would be public knowledge."

I just shook my head and laughed. "You have a point." My heart swelled in my chest. It still amazed me that I had this big, powerful, yet gentle and sweet man, in my life. That in less than a month I'd be his husband and he'd be mine. I touched his face with the tip of my index finger, running it across his cheek to his lips. "Do you know how much I love you?"

"Yeah, I do." He gently kissed my finger then clutched my hands, pressing them against his chest over his heart, and said confidently, "And, Danny, there is no Plan C."

SJD PETERSON, better known as Jo, hails from Michigan. Not the best place to live for someone who hates the cold and snow. When not reading or writing, Jo can be found close to the heater checking out NHL stats and watching the Red Wings kick a little butt. Can't cook, misses the clothes hamper nine out of ten tries, but is handy with power tools.

Visit Jo at http://www.facebook.com/SJD.Peterson;
http://sjdpeterson.blogspot.com/;
https://twitter.com/SJDPeterson;
and http://www.goodreads.com/author/show/4563849.S_J_D_Peterson.
Contact Jo at sjdpeterson@gmail.com.

http://www.dreamspinnerpress.com

A WHISPERING PINES RANCH NOVEL
BOOK II

QUINN'S
NEED

SJD PETERSON

http://www.dreamspinnerpress.com

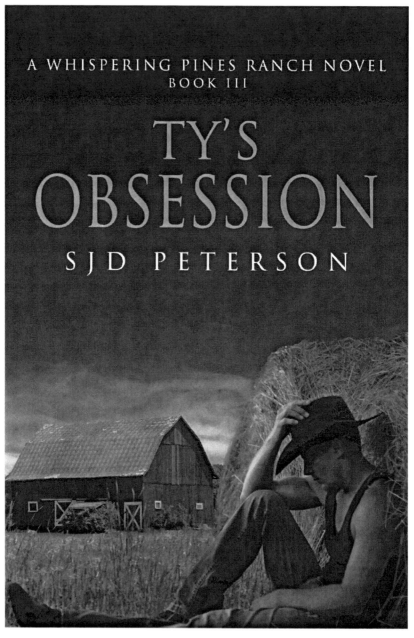

A WHISPERING PINES RANCH NOVEL
BOOK III

TY'S
OBSESSION

SJD PETERSON

WHISPERING PINES RANCH by SJD PETERSON

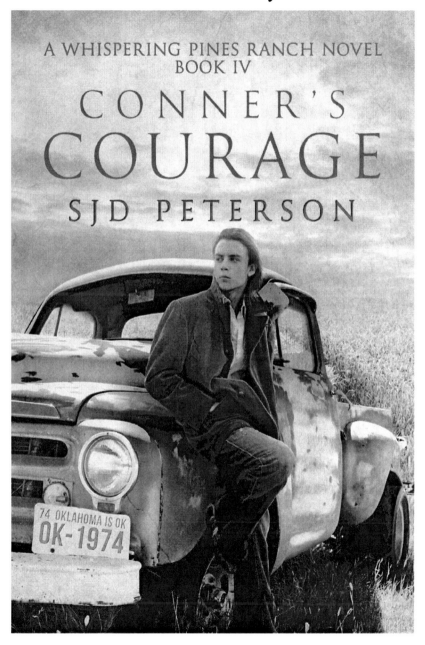

http://www.dreamspinnerpress.com

WHISPERING PINES RANCH by SJD PETERSON

A WHISPERING PINES RANCH NOVEL
BOOK V
JESS'S
JOURNEY
SJD PETERSON

http://www.dreamspinnerpress.com

Also from SJD PETERSON

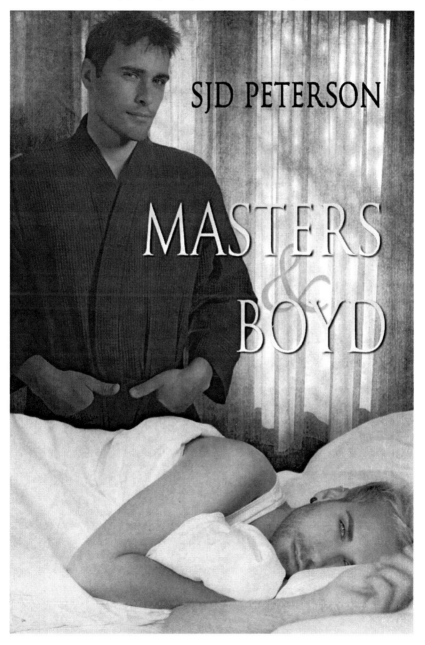

SJD PETERSON

MASTERS
&
BOYD

http://www.dreamspinnerpress.com

STRAWBERRIES
FOR DESSERT

MARIE SEXTON

Also from DREAMSPINNER PRESS

http://www.dreamspinnerpress.com

CPSIA information can be obtained
at www.ICGtesting.com
Printed in the USA
LVOW10s1513061216
516057LV00009B/1224/P

9 781623 803377